Didn't he trust h...
didn't trust her?

Jet was in a pickle, and had no choice but to take Coco up on that sofa offer.

"Fine," he said aloud as he trudged back to her front door, the snow and cold wind blasting his face and hands with its bitter sting. He hated nights like this, nights when Mother Nature reminded him of her power, and when memories of his childhood came crashing back. But most of all, he hated that the baby would now be a ward of the state and he would be the one to hand her over.

The irony was too real.

Life sure could stink at times, he thought, but before he was able to ring the bell, Coco swung open the door and handed him that shot of scotch.

"Thanks," he said, stepping forward.

"I saw you through the window and figured as much," she said, her voice low and sultry, feet bare, pretty little toes painted a bright pink.

No doubt about it, he was in for it now...

Dear Reader,

This is the last book for the Grant family. It features Doctor Coco Grant and Sheriff Jet Wilson, a character I introduced in previous Briggs books. The good sheriff never had a very prominent role until he spoke to me when I began to outline this book.

I couldn't ignore him. Not when I knew he would make such a great hero for Coco, who knows everything about animals, but absolutely nothing about babies. I decided to turn things around and have Jet be the one who can change a diaper, prepare formula and lull a fussy baby into sleep. It's all in his background, which he thought was his misfortune, but as it turns out it's one of his biggest assets.

I really loved writing about these characters and baby Lily, who will surely steal your heart. After all, she stole mine as soon as I met her. I happen to love babies, and this little darlin' is especially sweet. So get ready to fall in love not only with baby Lily, but with Jet Wilson, who just wants to do what's best for everyone involved.

It's really hard for me to say goodbye to the Grants, just as it was difficult to say goodbye to the Grangers, but I'm moving on to the Porter family, with four delightful stories planned beginning in 2018.

Till then, enjoy the Grants as they come together once again, along with those quirky townsfolk from Briggs, Idaho, to prove that love is all you need...and maybe a good snowplow.

Visit me on Facebook, maryleoauthor, and Twitter, @maryleoauthor.

Happy reading!

Mary

A BABY FOR
THE SHERIFF

—

Mary Leo

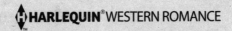

HARLEQUIN® WESTERN ROMANCE

PLEASE RECYCLE · THIS PRODUCT IS RECYCLABLE ·

Recycling programs
for this product may
not exist in your area.

ISBN-13: 978-0-373-75780-0

A Baby for the Sheriff

Copyright © 2017 by Mary Leo

All rights reserved. Except for use in any review, the reproduction or utilization of this work in whole or in part in any form by any electronic, mechanical or other means, now known or hereinafter invented, including xerography, photocopying and recording, or in any information storage or retrieval system, is forbidden without the written permission of the publisher, Harlequin Enterprises Limited, 225 Duncan Mill Road, Don Mills, Ontario M3B 3K9, Canada.

This is a work of fiction. Names, characters, places and incidents are either the product of the author's imagination or are used fictitiously, and any resemblance to actual persons, living or dead, business establishments, events or locales is entirely coincidental.

This edition published by arrangement with Harlequin Books S.A.

For questions and comments about the quality of this book, please contact us at CustomerService@Harlequin.com.

® and TM are trademarks of Harlequin Enterprises Limited or its corporate affiliates. Trademarks indicated with ® are registered in the United States Patent and Trademark Office, the Canadian Intellectual Property Office and in other countries.

HARLEQUIN®
™ www.Harlequin.com

Printed in U.S.A.

USA TODAY bestselling author **Mary Leo** grew up in south Chicago in the tangle of a big Italian family. She's worked in Hollywood, Las Vegas and Silicon Valley. Currently she lives in Las Vegas with her husband, author Terry Watkins, and their sweet kitty, Sophie. Visit her website at maryleo.com.

Books by Mary Leo

Harlequin Western Romance

A Cowboy in Her Arms
A Cowboy to Kiss

Harlequin American Romance

Falling for the Cowboy
Aiming for the Cowboy
Christmas with the Rancher
Her Favorite Cowboy
A Christmas Wedding for the Cowboy

Visit the Author Profile page
at Harlequin.com for more titles.

For darling Elena, who contacts me every day to see how I'm doing, who surprises me with thoughtful gifts and who is a constant delight.

And for my son, Rich, who fell in love with her.

Chapter One

The wine was poured. The fire burned bright in the hearth. Doctor Coco Grant, the town's vet, had painted her toenails, donned extra makeup, chosen her most seductive underwear—the blush lace panties and bra she'd bought anticipating this moment—slipped into her sexiest black dress and even shaved her legs.

All of it done in preparation for her date with Russ Knightly, the potential new mayor of Briggs, Idaho, and one of the most sought-after eligible bachelors for a hundred miles. At thirty-three, he would be the youngest mayor of Briggs, and the one man in the entire county whom Coco had lusted over for the past five years while he dated several other women. One of them he'd even proposed to. Fortunately for Coco, that engagement didn't last more than a few weeks.

Now it was Coco's turn...the woman he was meant to be with, the woman he would love like no other, the woman for whom he was about to fulfill all her sexual fantasies in one hot night, and the woman she hoped would one day be referred to as Doctor Coco Knightly, the mayor's wife. Her family, especially her brother, Carson, admired Russ. Carson had been sponsored by the Knightly Endowment for the Preservation of Western Culture when he had first started competing as a bronc rider in local rodeos.

Coco had been smitten ever since Russ, and a few other cowboys, rescued a small herd of wild horses trapped up in the Teton Mountains. Russ had risked his life to go up there and lead those animals out, under severe avalanche warnings for the area.

Ever since that moment, she thought Russ Knightly was a kindred spirit who loved and respected animals as much as she did. He was simply the bravest man alive, or at least the bravest man in Briggs, next to her brother and her dad, of course.

"I've been thinking about you all day," Russ said as he walked backward to her bedroom, pulling her along with one hand, the other caressing his glass of expensive scotch, a scotch that Coco had ordered online just for this occasion, a fifteen-year-old scotch she knew he would love.

"Me, too," she told him as she eagerly followed him, aroused by the mere idea of what was about to happen in her once lonely bedroom.

She and Russ had been dating for almost two months, thanks to an official introduction by her brother, but because of her schedule and his mayoral campaign, they hadn't found the time to take their relationship to the next level.

Tonight, they would break through all those levels with pure lust, pure sex and pure seduction. At twenty-nine, Coco hadn't really experienced a lot of sex, especially not the kind that Russ Knightly was noted for. She'd been too busy with her studies, volunteering and dreaming about Russ to care much about dating other guys.

But all that was in her past now. Tonight the floodgates were open, and each time he touched her a fire ignited that she didn't want to put out anytime soon.

Heck, Coco had even locked her little dog, Punky, a Yorkshire terrier, in the bathroom. For some reason she couldn't understand, Punky didn't seem to like Russ, and growled whenever he came close to Coco.

Well, there would be none of that tonight.

Tonight Coco and Russ would be so close they might need the Jaws of Life to pull them apart.

"I have plans for you, baby, plans for your body," he muttered in a deep voice.

She loved it when he called her *baby.*

"What kind of plans?" she teased, loving how he made her feel all tingly.

"Dirty plans that will make you blush whenever you think about our first night."

"I'm already blushing," she demurely said. "And I have my own plans."

That was a complete fabrication. The only plans she'd had that day were how to foal a breached horse and what kind of drugs she would administer to Helen Granger's horse, Tater, for the infection in his right front femur.

Russ stopped, pulled her in tight and kissed her. Although Coco's mind sometimes drifted whenever they kissed, she felt certain once they were in bed to-

gether her focus would laser in on the task at hand—
not that making love to Russ was a task. What she
meant was, once they were in bed together, nothing
else would matter and she'd be able to surrender to
the moment.

Of course it would be that way, she told herself.
He was the man she wanted to be with forever. The
man she'd dreamed about, longed for and pictured as
the father of her children.

Russ Knightly was her man, her guy, her Mr. Right.

As he pulled her in tighter and she felt the bulge of
his manhood press against her body, her heart raced,
and suddenly all she could think of was how this was
finally going to happen. She was going to make love
with her dream man. Life couldn't get any better if
it had been scripted.

Until the doorbell rang for her animal clinic downstairs. She'd only recently, in the last eight months,
finished construction on the two-thousand-foot expansion. She'd had proper ventilation installed, added
to the reception area and incorporated two large pens
for the livestock she inevitably took in. She'd been
thinking of hiring another doctor to help out, but so
far, she hadn't made the time to begin the search…a
fact she now found herself regretting.

Russ kept his lips pressed to hers as if he hadn't
heard it.

"I…I, um, I should get that," she mumbled while
his lips stuck to hers.

"Not tonight. Whoever it is will go away."

The bell rang again.

"Or not," she said, trying to disengage from him. It felt as though his lips were glued to hers and she couldn't unstick them.

"I…really…need…to…get…that."

He finally stepped back and Coco swore their lips popped apart. "You're not seriously going to leave me here like this while you answer the door."

He nodded down toward the bulge in his pants, which for some odd reason was no longer doing it for her. Not when she knew someone's animal could be in crisis.

"I'm sorry," she said, slipping out from his embrace, "but as much as I would like to, I can't ignore the bell. It wouldn't be right. If someone's trudged through all that snow and cold, I have no choice but to at least answer the door."

He glanced at his watch. "It's ten o'clock at night. Nobody just brings over their sick animal at this time of night without calling first."

"All the more reason why I need to get that. It's probably an emergency."

Coco ran a hand through her hair, placed her wineglass on the table and turned to dash down the stairs to answer the door.

The bell rang again.

"Persistent, aren't they?" he said, sounding resentful.

She turned back to him. "I'll only be a minute. I'm sure it's something minor and I'll be able to fix it in no time."

But Coco wasn't so sure. Usually whenever her doorbell rang this late, someone was leaving behind an unwanted or sick pet they could no longer care for. She flipped on the light switch in the stairwell and through the glass on the top half of the door caught the shadow of a woman wearing a puffy coat and hood as she walked away.

"Oh, shoot," she said aloud, knowing full well it was a drop-off. She already had a piglet named Jimmy, two baby goats, one puppy, two persnickety calico kittens, an adult tortoise named Tortie and two temperamental baby llamas taking shelter in her clinic. She'd find homes for all of them eventually, but at the moment, the farm animals were illegal within city limits, and if Sheriff Jet Wilson—who did everything by the book—learned about them, he'd issue her another fine on top of the last two she couldn't afford to pay. She'd spent all her savings on the expansion.

When she arrived at the bottom of the stairs, she grabbed the gray sweater that hung on a hook next to the door and slipped it on. Whatever was waiting for her on the other side of that door was more than likely going to require her standing out in the cold for a minute or two before she could wrangle it inside.

Good thing she still wore her shoes, albeit three-inch heels, but shoes nonetheless.

"Okay, what do we have this time?" she asked as she swung open the door expecting another goat or llama or…

Sheriff Jet Wilson fought his way back to the jail. The official white SUV, with the Briggs Sheriff's Department logo emblazoned on the two front doors, was fishtailing at almost every turn. The snow was piling up fast now, and driving was nearing impossible. Benny Snoots, the town's one and only official snowplow driver, worked as fast as he could, but the snow was just too much for him.

Russ Knightly, a man Jet Wilson didn't much like, promised two more snowplows if he was elected mayor, and on a night like this, Jet considered giving him his vote…or not.

If, on the other hand, Mayor Sally Hickman won again, Jet would make sure at least one more snowplow was on her agenda, and if it wasn't, he promised himself he'd take up the cause himself and add plowing capability to the front of the SUV.

When he finally pulled up in front of the small jailhouse, he parked curbside and got out. His very first step encased his cowboy boots in so much snow that it slipped inside his boots and made a mess of his nice warm woolen socks. He grabbed the bags of food that he'd picked up at Sammy's Smokehouse off the back seat, slammed the doors shut and headed for the front of the jail. None of the townsfolk knew he was living at the jail these days and no one needed to know.

A water pipe had burst in his apartment earlier that week, and until his landlord could get it fixed and repair the damage to the floor and the wall, Jet didn't have anywhere else to go…at least nowhere he could afford. All the rooms in this town were too pricey for him and, well, he didn't want to impose on what few friends he had.

Being relatively new to Briggs, having lived there

for less than two years, making friends had been tough. Especially since he'd ticked off Russ Knightly, who seemed to be a big deal in town, next to Carson Grant, the town's one and only rodeo hero. Jet admired Carson, and had met him a few times, but Russ was another story entirely. He hadn't meant to make him mad, but the guy had been doing seventy-five in a fifty-five-mile zone, had a taillight out and was missing his front license plate when Jet had pulled him over. Idaho required two license plates, no matter what kind of vehicle you drove, and besides, the guy had way too much attitude for Jet's liking.

Little had Jet known that Russ seemed to pull all the important strings in town, and in the state, for that matter, and when you were merely a small-town sheriff, those strings could get pretty tight.

In the end, his violations had somehow been dismissed, and Jet had ended up the bad guy.

Of course, at the moment, Jet didn't give a hoot. The jail suited him just fine, thank you very much. The bed in the cell was comfortable enough, and rarely used, so he thought he'd break it in for a few days.

He swung open the heavy front door, hit the light switch, slipped out of his bulky parka and cowboy hat, tugged off his boots and his wet socks, sat down at his desk inside his small office and tore open the bags of delicious-smelling barbecue. His mouth instantly watered in anticipation. He hadn't eaten all day, and his stomach had started aching about three hours ago from lack of food. The pungent smells filled the room as Jet cracked open a can of beer and took a long pull.

He was in for the night, and it felt good to finally be free of all responsibilities. He took a big bite of one of the beef ribs, ripping the meat off the bone with his teeth, groaned his delight and walked over to put his wet socks on the old radiator under the bank of windows so they could dry. All the blinds were closed, so no one could see him, not that there was anyone out there looking on a night like this. Still it gave him comfort to be hidden from view for a while. He walked back to the desk, took another big bite and was just about to sit down and settle in when the phone rang…his phone, in his pocket. The phone that he kept private, and only a handful of people had the number.

That phone rang.

The jailhouse phone had an all-night service for any emergency calls, but that wasn't ringing.

He felt the sigh that seemed to come up from his bare feet before he heard it expel from his throat as he pulled his phone out of his pocket and checked the screen.

Doctor Coco Grant's name lit up the black screen along with the picture he'd taken of her in front of her illegal goat pen inside her clinic.

Part of him didn't want to answer, but he knew if she was calling this late at night, it must be important.

Frankly, he didn't want to hear about "important" right now, not in the middle of what had to be the best barbecue ribs Sammy had ever created.

He chewed and swallowed.

"Hello," he reluctantly said into his phone.

"Hi, Sheriff. Sorry to bother you this late, but I've got a situation over here that requires your attention."

He glanced up at the large clock above the front door knowing perfectly well that whatever it was that required his attention would take him at least another hour or more and it was already going on ten thirty.

"Can I give it my attention over the phone? It's pretty nasty out there tonight, and it's late. Besides, if someone left you another goat or any other farm animal, there's nothing either one of us can do about it tonight."

"It's not a goat, Sheriff. It's a baby."

As he took another bite of a rib, sauce dripped down his fingers and landed on his shirt and lap— bright red sauce that stained everything it touched. He cursed under his breath as he tried to wipe it up.

"You don't have to get nasty about it," she said in his ear.

"No. I wasn't talking to you. It's just that… Look, let's call a truce for tonight. I don't care what kind of illegal baby critter someone left you. We can deal with it another time, just not right now."

"If you don't want to do your job, fine, but you should know it's not a critter of any kind this time. It's a baby, as in a human baby. A little girl named Lily. She's about two weeks old from what I can tell and in desperate need of a diaper change, which I think I can do with an old T-shirt. But some real diapers would be nice. And some formula, and a new outfit, cause she soiled this one and wrapping her in something of mine isn't a real option."

He didn't know what to say or how to respond. He'd never dealt with an abandoned baby before. He'd have to read up on it, or at the very least call someone over in Boise to give him a quick rundown of protocol.

"Hello. Hello. Hello. Are you there?" she said, sounding agitated.

He finally took a breath. "Did you say a baby girl?"

"Yes. An infant, and from what I can tell, the only note we have is written on the back of a restaurant receipt from Sammy's Smokehouse with Lily's name on it and nothing else."

He stood, raking a hand through his hair while trying to gather his thoughts. Then he said, "I'll be right over."

"WHY IS SHE crying so much?" Russ asked for the umpteenth time as he awkwardly held baby Lily by her head and butt, flying her back and forth like he was getting ready to propel her through the air. "Is she sick? Maybe she's got something really wrong with her?"

"Or maybe it's the way you're holding her. Haven't you held a baby before?"

Coco walked over and took Lily, carefully folding the baby into her arms. At once, Lily calmed down as Coco gently spoke to her and naturally bounced with each step, trying to soothe the fretful child.

"There has to be something wrong with her. She

smells horrible. I don't want to get too close, what with all the events I have coming up in the next week. I can't afford to be sick."

He was right about the events, at least five that she knew of, and three of them she would be attending alongside him.

So no, he couldn't get sick, but she really didn't think that baby Lily had anything physically wrong with her other than needing a diaper change and maybe a bottle.

Coco knew how to treat and care for animals, but what she knew about babies couldn't fill one page. She was going on instinct here, and what she'd seen her sisters do. Sure, she'd held their babies, but she'd never changed a diaper nor had she ever had to soothe the little darlings or feed them. She'd successfully avoided all of that...up until now.

"She's a baby. Babies poop and pee. It's not her fault she smells. She just needs her diaper changed."

"Can you do that?" His forehead furrowed as if the mere thought of changing a diaper made him nauseous.

"I could if I had a diaper or even an old T-shirt or a dishcloth, but I don't think I own any safety pins. We'll just have to bear it until the sheriff gets here with supplies."

"Well, you can at least strip her down and clean her up, then maybe wrap her in a clean blanket."

From the tortured look on Russ's face, Coco thought she should do just that, or what was left of her date night might end right now.

"Okay. Let me see what I can put together," she re-assured him. "Not that I wanted to call him in the first place—we could have simply called Child Welfare or the hospital or anyone other than Sheriff Wilson... even his deputy would have been better. There's no telling what that man might do with a baby."

"Don't be ridiculous. He'll do what he's been trained to do with an abandoned baby...whatever that is."

"You know how that man is with the animals that get left on my doorstep. I'm still paying the fines for keeping some of them longer than the city will allow. If it were up to him, he'd turn them all over to the ani-mal shelter in Idaho Falls, where they'd be put down if no one claimed them in seventy-two hours, sooner if they're overcrowded. The man has no heart."

"He's just doing his job, as I'm sure he will with Billy."

"Her name is Lily. Why can't you remember that?"

"I don't know. Does it really matter? She can't un-derstand me."

Lily let out a blood-curdling wail.

"I actually think she can. Or at least she doesn't like the tone of your voice."

Coco pulled the baby in tighter.

"Okay. Okay," he whispered. "Is this better?"

Coco bounced Lily and she quieted down. The little darling seemed to like motion, so Coco kept it going.

"Yes, thank you."

Coco walked to her bedroom with Lily fussing on Coco's shoulder, but she seemed to want to calm herself. She squeaked and cooed instead of wailing, a definite improvement. Once inside her bedroom, Coco contemplated putting Lily down on her bed, the bed she'd bought new silky sheets for, and sprayed with perfume, and surrounded with candlelight. The bed she and Russ would make love on until her body ached and she cried out for more.

The bedroom that had been set up for sin.

That bedroom where she now flipped the switch for the overhead light and blew out the candles…at least for now.

She carefully laid squirming baby Lily down on the scented bed while trying to soothe her with soft-spoken words, which weren't working. She walked to her bathroom and prepared a couple warm wash-cloths and then brought along a couple fluffy clean towels—new towels that she'd also picked up for the shower she and Russ would take together after hours of making love.

So much for all her sexy plans.

Of course, the night was still relatively young. Anything could happen.

Placing one towel under Lily and keeping one handy to wrap her in, Coco began to undress the lit-tle sweetheart, who had stopped fussing when Coco started singing the first song that came into her head, "Happy Birthday."

"I'd offer to help," Russ said, coming up behind her, "but I'm horrible with kids, especially babies. Plus, I don't know the first thing about changing a diaper."

"And you think I do?" Coco said as she gently wiped

off Lily's soiled bottom. Russ made a few disgusted grunts and turned away.

Coco knew enough from birthing livestock to keep hold of Lily's arms while she cleaned her. Newborns of any kind liked to be touched and held whenever something else was happening to them. This one little action seemed to soothe her, exactly like it soothed a foal.

"You're a woman," Russ announced as if that fact had any relevance in this situation.

"What's that supposed to mean?"

"It's in your DNA. Besides, you deal with babies all the time."

"There's a big difference between a puppy or a foal and a little baby girl, an abandoned baby girl. Poor sweetheart doesn't know what to think…do you, sweet Lily?"

Lily made a couple complaints, but then settled when Coco began singing "Happy Birthday" again.

"Where's that sheriff? He should've been here by now." Russ walked up behind Coco and ran his hands down her body. Normally a great sensation, and a real turn-on, but not while Coco was trying to clean up baby poop. "We need to pick up where we left off."

She moved away from him, leaning in closer to Lily, who was now nice and clean and smelling of new baby, a delightful scent if there ever was one.

"I don't know if that's possible tonight, Russ. The mood has sort of been broken."

Coco swaddled Lily as best she could inside the soft white towel, then picked her up, cradling her tight against her chest, her little rosebud mouth suckling the air.

"Not really. I know how we can get it back again."

"How?"

He leaned in and kissed her with one of those sinful kisses that might have brought her to her knees… if it wasn't for the warm trickle of liquid that now ran down between her breasts.

SHERIFF WILSON WASN'T about to drive over to Dr. Grant's clinic without all the supplies she'd asked for, and then some. He'd taken care of enough babies in his life to know exactly what she needed. Plus, he knew enough about the system to know that the chances of his being able to drop off a baby with the appropriate authorities at this time of night, with all this snow, were slim to none. After he'd changed out of his uniform into more casual wear, he'd made a few phone calls, and the only words of encouragement he'd gotten were *keep her warm*.

Driving down Main Street was proving to be a challenge, despite his being the only actual vehicle on the road. Even Travis Granger, who maneuvered his red sleigh and Clydesdales, picking up any stranded pedestrians, was having a time of it. The two men nodded to each other as they passed, silently acknowledging that Briggs was in for it tonight.

By the time Sheriff Wilson tried to pull his SUV curbside on Main Street, then trudge up to the glass front door of Whipple's One Stop and push on the bell that rang inside the Whipple apartment upstairs, he felt the tension intensify in his neck and shoulders. Jet braced himself for what was sure to be the third degree from Cindy Whipple, proprietor and one of the biggest town gossips. Not only was she a gossip, but she had town radar and could usually figure out what someone was trying desperately to hide. She had the uncanny ability to guess exactly what was going on before anyone could tell her the truth.

A sweet woman with a heart of gold, but she couldn't keep a secret if God came down and asked her personally.

Within moments, a soft light came on inside the store, illuminating the frozen-food section located in the back. Jet and Cindy locked eyes for a moment before she disappeared behind the produce shelves.

When the glass door finally swung open, bells chiming overhead, Cindy Whipple greeted him wearing a fuzzy red robe and matching slippers. Her short white hair stuck out in strange angles, as if she'd just come out of a windstorm, and her horn-rimmed glasses were askew on her wizened face. But her lips were perfectly smeared with red lipstick. Ms. Whipple never went out in public without her bright red lipstick in place. And, apparently, that went for answering the door late at night.

"Sheriff Wilson! What in blazes are you doing out here so late? Did somebody die? Is there a big accident somewhere and you need medical supplies? Because I can give you a deal you won't believe."

"No, nothing like that, but is it possible that you

could open your store for me? I know it's late, ma'am, but I would really appreciate getting a few things."

"I take it this is some kind of emergency, or you wouldn't be standing here. Are you going to tell me what happened or is it a secret?"

He decided to play along. "Yes, it's a secret, and I can't tell anyone about it. Not even you."

"Me? I'm Fort Knox," she said with a chuckle.

If only that were true.

"Good, because I'm depending on you not to ask me any questions. I promised I wouldn't say a word."

"Absolutely. Not one question. Not a word. My lips are sealed." She slipped two fingers across her pursed lips, as if she was zipping them up. "Now, what do you need?"

He was hoping he could get out of there without giving her any details. At this point, that was about all he could hope for.

"Baby formula, newborn diapers, a few of those onesies, some undershirts, a couple baby bottles, nipples, a little knit hat and blankets, lots of those small baby blankets," he told her all in one breath. "Oh, and baby wipes, several containers of baby wipes."

Her eyes went wide, and she straightened up her glasses. "Now, why on earth are you in here buying up baby supplies?"

"You promised no questions. I'm depending on you."

"But…"

He tilted his head and gave her a look.

She took a step back and let out a big sigh. "Okay,

okay." Then she quickly went about gathering up all the supplies, placing them on the counter.

After a moment she yelled from across the store, "A boy or girl?"

"Why would that matter?" He knew she was fishing.

"Just want to know if I should pick up blue or pink blankets and onesies."

"Yellow or green will work."

"Fine!" she said, but he could tell this secret thing was killing her.

Soon, the counter was littered with baby things. Fortunately, Jet knew enough about newborns to know they didn't need rattles, teething toys or the high chair she'd stuck next to the counter.

In the end, he managed to get exactly what he needed, even picking up a thermal onesie suitable for winter weather and some sort of soft travel bassinet Cindy had sung the praises of. He'd have gotten a car seat as well, but it wasn't sized for an infant. Other than that, Whipple's One Stop truly had everything he needed for baby Lily.

He was just about to compliment Cindy Whipple when she interrupted. "I've thought about the expectant moms in town, and I've accounted for all of them. I think it's someone from out of town. Am I right?"

"I can't say," Jet told her, swallowing his praise.

"Is it one of our teens? Some poor girl who has managed to keep her pregnancy a secret, even from her parents? I bet it's Roseland Cooper, or maybe Jennifer Wells…or maybe it's not either of them. I bet it's one of them Century sisters, maybe Bess or Dani. Them girls always were wild…no mother to raise 'em and a dad who didn't value nothin' but his next drink. Just because they're of age now doesn't mean they've got a lick of common sense. Neither one of 'em could settle. Always movin' 'round the country."

Jet knew the Century sisters well, especially Dani Century, but he didn't want to think about her now. That was over a long time ago, and bringing up her name only reminded him of a time in his life he didn't want to relive, especially not tonight.

"They don't live here anymore, Mrs. Whipple. They both headed out months ago."

"Oh, that's right. Time gets away from me," she said as she bagged everything. "You're not going to tell me, are you?"

"I can't, remember?"

"But it's a baby. Nobody can hide a baby…unless…" She sucked in air and put her hand over her mouth.

"Unless what? Mrs. Whipple? What are you thinking?"

She leaned in closer over the counter, and whispered, "Some out-of-towner abandoned a baby at the jail, didn't they? And your deputy is caring for it right now while you're in here getting supplies. Child Welfare can't do nothing about it in all this snow, and the road to the hospital is probably closed by now, so you're stuck. I bet that's it. You can tell me. My lips are sealed. Fort Knox."

But Jet didn't answer. Instead he picked up the two overflowing bags wondering how on earth Cindy

Whipple could have gotten so close to the truth. The woman had a sixth sense about these things, and if Jet hung around any longer he was sure she'd figure out the baby's name, gender and, even worse, that the baby was abandoned on Doctor Grant's doorstep.

As he walked out of the store, he contemplated hiring Mrs. Whipple as a special investigator. Not that he ever could or would, but having her work with him seemed a lot smarter than having her working against him…of that he had no doubt.

Chapter Two

"Are we ever happy to see you," Russ Knightly said as he opened the front door to Coco's private residence above her clinic. The door to her clinic sat right next to her private apartment door, but despite the sign above it that touted Paws & Tails Animal Clinic, the sheriff knew her patrons managed to get the two doors confused, just as he had the first time he'd stopped by. They looked exactly alike but for the sign, which, in his opinion, should have been placed on the door itself.

Russ's clothes looked disheveled and he wore a harried look on his cover-model face, as if the normally cavalier mayoral candidate had reached his breaking point. Even his habitually groomed dark hair was tousled.

Jet could only think of one question: Why was *he* here?

The shock of seeing Russ standing in Doctor Grant's doorway instead of Doctor Grant herself threw Sheriff Wilson off his game for a moment. Of all the men in this town, Russ Knightly was the last person he ever thought he'd see anywhere near

Coco Grant. For one thing, he'd thought she was a smart woman…but unless there was a really good reason for this lunkhead to be answering her door at this time of night, Jet had sorely misjudged Coco's common sense.

"I got a call from Doctor Grant, but if you're already here, I'll just drop these off with you." He shoved the bag of baby things into Russ's hands, and placed a bigger bag of diapers and baby wipes just inside the doorway. "I'll be on my way before the snow gets any deeper."

Then he turned to go, angry that he'd been used as an errand boy.

"No. Wait. Aren't you going to take the baby?"

The sheriff turned back around, detecting a hint of angst in Russ's normally brazen voice. "Can't. There's nobody to care for her tonight."

Jet proceeded down the three front steps off the wide porch, until Russ called to him again. The man had actually followed him, carrying both bags of baby things. Did Russ really think he was going to stop him from leaving?

"Well, we certainly can't take care of it. We're not authorized, but I know for a fact that you are. It's your duty as town sheriff to take custody of this baby."

Jet hesitated at the bottom of the steps on the snowy sidewalk and contemplated his options. According to the local newspaper, the *Teton Valley Gazette*, Russ Knightly was beating Mayor Sally Hickman by ten points. If he became mayor, he could make Jet's life miserable, and even replace him if he so chose.

Despite all his complaints, Sheriff Jet Wilson loved

his job and didn't want to start over again in some other town...at least not yet.

"You're right about that, Mr. Knightly. I must have been mistaken. I thought you and Doctor Grant wanted to keep that poor, destitute, abandoned child overnight, which would be fine, according to the law, as long as I approved it. Which I do."

"Well, don't, because we do not want to keep the baby overnight. We want you to take her. Coco...I mean, Doctor Grant, and I have other plans."

Jet got it loud and clear. This charming snake and Doctor Grant were in a relationship. Russ might as well have sucker punched him right in the jaw. It would have made more sense than this tawdry relationship.

As much as it pained Jet, he walked back up the three steps, past Russ Knightly, then began walking up the flight of stairs to the doctor's private residence, an apartment he'd never seen before, but had thought about many times.

"You could have carried some of this stuff, ya know," Russ complained behind Jet as the two men made their way up the steps.

"I sure could have," Jet said, offering no excuse, listening to Russ grunt as he tried to maneuver the steep stairs.

Jet's guilt kicked in and he was about to turn back around and grab one of the bags from Russ when the door opened to Doctor Grant's apartment.

She looked absolutely gorgeous, almost beatific, as if she was no longer human, but rather an angel that had come down from heaven. It was all there in her smile, a radiant, joyful smile not really intended for Jet, but coming from deep within her.

Seeing the doctor standing in the doorway, with that tiny baby cradled in her arms, wearing a beautiful black dress that hugged all her curves, her short-cropped, almost black hair hugging her face, showing off that lovely long neck of hers, earrings gently dusting her bare shoulders and the low light from her apartment bathing her body in its warm glow, took Jet's breath away. Her steel blue eyes seemed brighter, her lips fuller, and that chiseled nose set everything off making her look regal. Doctor Coco Grant always stood up straight, proud of her six-foot height, which Jet loved considering he cleared six foot four easy.

No woman had ever had that kind of impact on him before. The world might as well have stopped spinning.

For the first time in his adult life, he knew what it meant to be tongue-tied. It was all he could do to keep from blabbing like a schoolboy.

"Thanks for coming out, Sheriff. I know it's late, but we didn't know what else to do," the angel said, her voice low and enthralling.

"I...um..."

"Excuse me," Russ said from just behind Jet, then nudged him out of the way. "But this stuff is heavy."

That knocked Jet back into reality...the reality of an abandoned baby cuddled up against Doctor Grant, with bare shoulders exposed to the cold of the stairway.

Jet cleared his tight throat. "Not a problem," he told Doctor Grant. "I picked up a few things on my way over."

"More like the whole store," Russ muttered.

All of a sudden, the baby started wailing. Jet figured it was the grating sound of Russ's voice that set her off.

Smart baby, Jet thought.

"Why don't you let me get some clothes on that little darlin' while you make her a bottle. We can talk about how you found her after we get her settled," Jet said.

From the look on Doctor Grant's face, he could tell she hadn't expected him to know much about babies.

"Are you sure?" she tentatively asked. "Because, I mean…"

But Jet had already taken the tiny bundle wrapped in a fuzzy white towel into his arms. She felt as light as a feather as he spoke to her in a soothing voice and gently rocked her. At once the wailing turned into tiny whimpers.

"How'd you do that?" Coco asked, but Jet wasn't in the mood to answer her question. Instead he asked one of his own.

"Any bruises on the child?"

He walked past her and into the spacious apartment and immediately noticed all the lit candles on just about every flat surface in the large rooms, plus the open bottles of wine and scotch on the dining table that still held the remnants of what had to be a romantic dinner for two. A large bouquet of roses, undoubtedly a gift from her shining knight, sat in a clear glass vase in the center of the table.

Sheriff Jet Wilson could only imagine the disruption this little girl must have caused. He did a mental snicker.

"None that I could see," the doctor answered using her official voice. "She looks well cared for, and she's the appropriate size and weight for a two-week-old infant. I looked it up online."

"That's good. Now, where can I change her?"

"In my bedroom, down the hall on your right."

Jet picked one of the bags of essentials that Russ had dropped on the floor and went off to make little baby Lily a bit more comfortable in this uncomfortable situation.

"Can one of you please bring in the other bag?" Jet asked, not turning back around. He assumed Russ would carry in the bulky bag, and the less he saw and spoke to that man, the better.

Just last week he thought he'd seen Russ locking lips with a petite blonde woman over in Jackson Hole, Wyoming, a town less than thirty minutes from Briggs. Jet had been there for a meeting with law enforcement officials when he spotted Russ through a restaurant window cozying up with a woman Jet had never seen before. And from the way they'd been eyeing each other, Jet had assumed they were an item.

Apparently he'd been wrong.

Apparently Russ Knightly liked to spread his affections around.

"You wouldn't be taken in by that kind of behavior, would you, Lily?"

She blinked and pushed her spindly legs out from under the towel. He could tell she didn't particularly like that heavy towel over her. Jet put her down on the bed, opened the box of diapers, pulled one out and quickly slipped it under Lily's bottom and fastened it. Then he grabbed a white side-snap undershirt and slipped that on her. She at once looked much more comfortable and happy.

"There, now you can relieve yourself at will, and no one will be the wiser."

Her little arms reached up as she let out a soft wail. "Aw, sweet cakes, don't be cryin'. We're gonna fix you up with a bottle, and I promise you, you'll be well taken care of. No need to make a fuss."

As he soothed Lily, his mind wandered back to Russ and Jackson Hole, pondering whether or not the good doctor knew about the other woman or, for that matter, if the other woman knew about Doctor Grant.

And if both women knew, were they okay with it?

Call him old-fashioned, but in Jet's world, a relationship consisted of two people who only had eyes for each other.

Unfortunately, so far, those kinds of old-fashioned ideas hadn't panned out so well. He kept falling for the wrong women, but *dang it*, after his last broken heart, he'd promised himself he would never do that again.

Until the next time.

"Seems like you've got it covered," Doctor Grant said from behind him, her statement confusing him for a moment.

"Yes… I mean…you are referring to baby Lily, right?"

She came around and sat on the edge of the bed,

facing him. Her forehead mirrored her confusion. "What else would I be referring to?"

He needed to change the subject, and fast, as he slipped Lily into a warm, long-sleeved, bunny-covered sleeper gown and zipped it closed. "Is that bottle coming soon?"

She nodded. "Right here," she said. "I can feed her." She held out her arms, but Jet was reluctant to give Lily up. Instead, he gently picked her up and cradled her in his arms. She felt warm and delicate against his chest, and he had to get over the thought that she might break if he held her too tight. It had been a while, a long while, since he'd held a two-week-old baby, but he had no problem remembering exactly what to do.

"Just point me to a comfortable chair, and we'll be fine."

"You want to feed Lily?"

"Sure," he told her, swiping the bottle, testing the heat of the formula on the inside of his wrist, then gently enticing Lily to take it. She fussed, and wouldn't suckle no matter how he tried to encourage her. "Maybe she's used to her mama's breast, and this won't work. If that's true, we really have a problem."

He glanced over at Doctor Grant, whose breasts just happened to be at eye level and looking quite tempting spilling over that low-cut neckline.

"Well, don't look at me," she said, immediately standing.

"I wasn't looking… I mean… I couldn't help but see…" He stopped and took a deep breath, slowly letting it out. "I only meant this could be a real problem if she doesn't take the bottle."

Jet kept trying, but Lily kept making a face and crying. He could feel the tension building down the back of his neck and in his shoulders. He never even considered that she wouldn't take a bottle, and now he felt foolish for being so naive.

"You brought two kinds of bottles. Maybe she'll take the other one. It's worth a try," Doctor Grant said.

She left the bedroom and he followed right behind, grateful that Cindy Whipple had sold him both types of bottles. If this worked, he'd have to go back and kiss her!

"So, everything's good and you're getting ready to leave with Lily?" Russ said to Sheriff Wilson as he and Coco headed for the kitchen. Russ sat on the sofa in the open living room, sipping on a drink, seemingly waiting for all this baby fuss to end so he could get on with his night.

"Not yet," Jet said, trying to dismiss the vision of Russ and that blonde, seeming so cozy.

"Lily won't take her bottle," Doctor Grant told him, sounding concerned.

"Maybe she's not hungry," Russ answered, as if he knew something about babies. "A hungry baby will eat."

"Where did you hear that?" Jet asked, but kept heading for the kitchen with Doctor Grant.

"I just made it up, but it sounds perfectly reasonable."

Jet couldn't help an eye roll. Fortunately, only Lily could see him, and when he gazed down at her, she seemed to appreciate the gesture as she sucked on her fist.

"Apparently you don't know much about babies. According to Sheriff Wilson, they're particular, especially if they've only been nursed. She may only accept a breast," Doctor Grant told him, as she rinsed the other bottle, the one with a nipple that looked more like a woman's breast.

"Then go find her one. There must be several women in this town who are nursing their babies."

Doctor Grant stopped what she was doing and stared at Russ. "You're kidding, right?"

"Well, what's the alternative?"

"We have another bottle. It has a different nipple," Jet said.

"And if that doesn't work?"

"Pray that it does," Doctor Grant said, her voice firm and filled with agitation. "Because if it doesn't, we're all in for a world of trouble."

Lily began wailing again, louder than ever. Doctor Grant took the bottle from Jet and sped up the procedure.

Russ abruptly stood. "Well, I can see that the two of you have this covered, so I'm going to be on my way," he shouted over Lily's protest. "If you need anything, anything at all, don't hesitate to call."

"You're leaving? Now?" Doctor Grant asked, as if his departure took her by surprise. Jet's only surprise was that Russ hadn't left when Lily first arrived.

"Sorry, baby, but I've got a lot to do tomorrow, especially if the snow keeps falling like it is," Russ told Doctor Grant. "It proves my point that Sally Hickman isn't fit to be mayor. When I'm the mayor there will be more than enough snowplows to keep our roads cleared."

He shrugged into his coat that had hung on a hook by the door.

Doctor Grant handed Jet the new bottle, which she'd filled with the contents of the other bottle. Then she walked over to Russ. "But I thought we… I thought you and I…"

Then they disappeared out into her stairway, closing the door, leaving the sheriff to tend to the more important person in the room: baby Lily.

ONCE RUSS KNIGHTLY made up his mind about something, he was the type of man who couldn't be budged…a trait that under normal circumstances, Coco admired…just not tonight.

He couldn't get out of there fast enough. He'd left in such a hurry, she hadn't even gotten the chance to kiss him goodbye before he was out the door and down the stairs.

"Are you sure you want to leave in all this snow? You might get stuck and have to walk back here, anyway," she called after him from the open doorway, having followed him down to the front door of her clinic.

Without even turning around, he said, "I've got four-wheel drive, and a snowplow on the front of my truck. I can get through anything."

And in the next few seconds he jumped into his oversize truck, turned over the ignition, lowered the plow and took off into the night.

She could have been upset as she closed the door, might have even thought that he'd been rude to leave so abruptly in the middle of things. She even could have decided that just maybe she might be dating the wrong man. But all she could focus on was the silence…the absolute and complete silence.

She quickly ascended the stairs to her apartment, wondering about baby Lily and worrying about the sheriff. Would he call the local hospital asking how to set up a volunteer nursing mom for Lily? Not that she knew exactly how that would work for an actual baby. She'd set it up for infant livestock before, but that was with the cooperation of local ranchers…

When she finally opened the door, somewhat out of breath from her rush to learn the truth, emotion gripped the back of her throat. She couldn't help the tears that cascaded down her cheeks.

"Oh, my gosh! She's taking it?" she whispered, fingers wiping her tears away. Seeing that tiny baby, eagerly drinking the bottle of formula, nestled in Sheriff Wilson's strong arms, while he took up all the space on her tan-colored overstuffed chair, was almost more than Coco could take in. For all his bluster, Coco now knew he was warm and fuzzy on the inside.

And as a bonus, Punky had curled up at Sheriff Wilson's feet, and aside from momentarily picking up his tiny head to watch Coco come back into the apartment, he seemed as though he wasn't about to budge.

"Hope you don't mind, but I let your dog out of the bathroom. I heard it whining so I figured it wanted out."

"Meet Punky. And he usually doesn't trust men. Did you give him a cookie or something?"

"Nope, just a little lovin'. He was lonely."

Punky normally didn't like strangers and tended to keep his distance. Heck, he didn't even like Russ, so this was some sort of miracle to say the least.

She almost couldn't believe what lay right before her eyes, and wondered if Russ could have been so gentle and loving with Lily if the sheriff hadn't shown up. Maybe that accounted for Russ's early retreat... He'd felt intimidated by the sheriff and would have been as compassionate if he'd only gotten the chance. Russ was a compassionate and caring man. He'd merely been in a hurry to beat the snow or he would be sitting in that very chair right now instead of the sheriff...who she had absolutely nothing in common with.

Except for baby Lily.

But other than that, they were as different as rain and sunshine.

"And what about Lily? Did you give her some lovin', as well?"

"It was just a matter of getting everything lined up right. The little sweetheart here was hungry. That tummy of hers probably hurt, plus I think it took her a while to settle into not having her mama feeding her. I don't want to speculate on why a woman gives up her baby, but whatever the reason, it sure is tough on the child."

"That goes for animals, as well. They get depressed, sometimes to the point of not wanting to eat. Plus, they cry a lot."

"Exactly like Lily."

"Well, she's not crying now."

"She's one content little girl who's getting sleepy. But I have to make sure she doesn't have any gas in that tummy of hers before she sleeps."

Coco watched as six feet four inches of muscled alpha male expertly tucked tiny baby Lily onto his receiving blanket–covered shoulder and rubbed her back as she squirmed and fretted over the loss of her food. Within moments a couple of hearty burps erupted, and Sheriff Wilson once again cradled Lily in his arms to feed her the rest of her bottle.

"Seems like you've done this a few times before," Coco told him, amazed at his gentleness and ease with Lily. She was certain she'd be all nerves and frets if she had to feed her. Feeding a kitten or a baby goat or an abandoned foal was one thing, but a fragile baby was something entirely different.

"A few," he told her, but she could tell he didn't want to talk about it.

That never stopped her before. "Younger brothers and sisters?"

"None."

"Nieces and nephews?"

"No siblings of any age."

Coco perched herself on the edge of the sofa, intrigued now. "Then how…"

"One of the families I lived with consisted of a baby and a toddler, along with several other children. The older kids, like me, knew how to take care of themselves, but neither the baby nor the toddler got very much attention, which caused them to cry a lot. It was merely a matter of necessity. In order for me to get any of my homework done, I learned how to keep them content."

"Where were their parents?"

"Like me, and like Lily here, their parents, for whatever reason, had abandoned them."

Coco's heart instantly shattered. She'd had no idea. "So you grew up in foster care?"

"Yep. From the time I was six years old, but that's not anything to concern yourself with. What we need to think about now—" his voice spiraled down into a whisper "—is Lily."

"The snow hasn't let up at since you got here," she whispered, thankful that Lily had finally fallen asleep. "I know you want to get her to Child Welfare or maybe to Valley Hospital, but the roads look treacherous."

"What are you proposing?" He asked the question, but didn't take his eyes off Lily.

She knew the sheriff was a stickler for the law, but she was hopeful that maybe he could bend the rules if she framed her idea exactly right. Besides Lily, her menagerie of animals downstairs was definitely not legal within city limits. Maybe if she offered to keep Lily for the night, he wouldn't go snooping around her clinic, and even if he did, he'd let her slide without a fine…at least for now.

"Since it's not safe out there for either you or Lily, you both can stay here for the night…if you want. Of course, I'm not trying to step on your toes when it comes to your authority. All I'm saying is, it's a long way to Valley Hospital and then back to your apartment. Instead, I can put Lily down in her soft bassinet on my bed for the night and make up the sofa for you. I have a spare bedroom, but it's for storage."

He thought about it for a moment, as if his brain had to wrap itself around the idea that her proposal might come with illegal strings he couldn't see.

"While you think about that," she said, "can I get you anything to drink? Water? Coffee? Milk?"

"Actually, I'd take a shot of that scotch if I was going to stay. It's been one heck of a night on a lot of counts." He stood. "But I can't stay. I tell you what. I'll leave Lily in your care for the night, but I should get going while I can still do that. I'll come by to pick her up in the morning once the roads are clear and I know for certain who will take her."

"You don't know that yet?"

"No. With the weather being what it is, the person I spoke to wasn't really sure how to handle it."

No way was Coco willing to let that baby go under those ambiguous circumstances.

"Then I'd be more than happy to take care of her tonight, and again, you're more than welcome to stay, as well."

"Thanks for the offer of your sofa." He gazed over at it, looking skeptical.

"Okay, so maybe you wouldn't be comfortable on my sofa. But if you slept on your side and bent your knees, five feet would be a perfectly acceptable fit."

"I appreciate the offer, but that SUV can get through just about anything. Now, let's get Lily settled in her bed."

Coco picked up Lily's cloth bassinet by the handles and made her way to the bedroom, where she placed it on the bed. Then, ever so carefully, the sheriff put Lily down on her back and expertly swaddled her with the blankets. Lily didn't even stir, but let out a long sigh.

Then he did something she'd seen her own dad do a million times to each of his children, always feeling the love her dad had for his family. The only difference now was what the sheriff said...

He leaned over and gently kissed baby Lily on the forehead, tenderly stroked the top of her head and whispered, "Sleep well, Lily. You're safe now."

Then he exited the room, leaving Coco to wonder: *Who are you and what have you done with by-the-book Sheriff Wilson?*

WHEN JET STEPPED back outside into the quiet night, leaving the warmth of Doctor Grant and baby Lily behind, the cold wind instantly sent a shiver down his spine. The thought of trying to drive through all this heavy snow only to get back to the drafty, lonely jail made him a combination of angry and sad.

Angry at himself for not taking the doctor up on her kind offer to sleep on her sofa, and sad that his life had come to sleeping inside a jail cell on a hard cot.

He shook his head as he made his way to his rig, which was somehow completely packed in snow. Still, he told himself if Russ could make it out of there, so could he.

One problem.

He would need a good-sized shovel to dig his way out. It looked as though a snowplow had purposely shoved snow all around his SUV, making it impossible for him to get out.

But who would do such an inconsiderate thing to the sheriff's rig?

At this point it didn't matter. What did matter was that he'd made a big deal about not spending the night with the doctor.

He corrected himself. Not *with* the doctor, but *at* the doctor's apartment. Was that the reason he didn't take her up on her offer of the sofa? Didn't he trust himself? Maybe he didn't trust her? If she and Russ had an "open relationship," would she try to seduce him?

He told himself that was plain silly.

He'd merely done the stand-up thing and left. Nothing more to it.

But now he was in a pickle, and had no choice but to take her up on that sofa offer.

"Fine," he said aloud as he trudged back to her front door, the snow and cold wind blasting his face and hands with its bitter sting. He hated nights like this, nights when Mother Nature reminded him of her power, and when memories of his childhood came crashing back. He wished he could talk to Lily's mom and tell her of the life that Lily more than likely would have. He'd like to somehow help Lily's mom with whatever reason brought her to abandoning her child. But most of all, he hated that Lily would now be a ward of the state and he would be the one to hand her over.

The irony was too real. By the time he'd graduated from high school he'd lived with twelve different families. Most of them were good people, but a few of them were borderline abusive or simply neglectful. Those were the kinds of households that he hoped Lily would never run across, but he knew the odds were stacked against her. Once she went into the system, there was no telling who would be her temporary parents.

Life sure could stink at times, he thought as he made his way back up the three steps to Doctor Grant's front porch, but before he was able to ring the bell for her apartment, she swung open the door and handed him that shot of scotch.

"Thanks," he said after he drank it down. "I really needed that."

"I figured as much," she said, her voice low and sultry, feet bare, pretty little toes painted a bright pink.

No doubt about it, he was in for it now.

Chapter Three

"I know these animals legally aren't supposed to be here, but there was nowhere else I could take them, especially after it started snowing," Coco told the sheriff as he helped her clean out their cages and pens.

Coco had slipped out of her lacy black dress, and instead donned jeans, rubber boots and an oversize red plaid shirt. She wore rubber gloves and had offered a pair of gloves to the sheriff, which he surprisingly took. She'd set up one of her many portable baby monitors, which she used for her animals, inside her bedroom, so she had baby Lily in her sights at all times.

As for the sheriff's part, he'd left his gun holstered and locked in a dresser drawer in the spare bedroom, his badge and cream-colored cowboy hat sat on a side table next to her sofa.

Medium-sized cages lined one wall of the room, where sibling calico kittens played with a brown-and-white bulldog puppy, who eagerly rolled around with each of them, while a large tortoise watched the activities from the shelter of its hard shell. Fortunately, aside from the need of an occasional heat lamp and a meal of greens and maybe a strawberry or two, a tortoise was low maintenance. Unlike the rest of her critters, which required not only basic needs but some loving and human interaction. Otherwise they'd never be comfortable around people.

The area smelled of a combination of manure, fresh hay and animal fur, a scent that had lost its impact on Coco some time ago. Since her renovation, this part of the clinic was now separated from her apartment on the second floor of the original main building. This new clinic took up most of the empty lot that had been behind her house. She'd bought this property precisely because she knew she'd be able to expand her business. The closest house on her street was at least fifty yards away.

"I understand," the sheriff said as he scooped up goat dung and hay from the large pen at the end of the large room.

Those two words caught her by complete surprise as she stared at him and dumped the waste material into a big plastic trash can.

"Thanks," she told him, but she wanted to give him a big hug.

"Don't tell me you take care of all these guys by yourself?"

The piglet and all the other critters required time and care. She could never do it alone.

"Not exactly. One of my neighbors, Drew Gillian, helps out whenever she can. Normally she'll take in the cats and a couple dogs if we have them, but this time, she already has two pups and a kitten. I couldn't burden her with any more, so I'm keeping them here for a few days, at least until the weather clears up."

"You did what you had to do, Doctor Grant," he said, sounding official. This new attitude of his had to stop if they were going to make it through the night without her thinking that perhaps the sheriff was redeemable.

"Why don't you call me Coco," she told him, wanting to be on more friendly terms. After all, the man was helping her clean out the cages for animals that he knew being here were completely illegal.

He gazed over at her, a smile lighting up his normally stern-looking face. "And you can call me Jet, at least for tonight."

"And after tonight?" She stopped cleaning and looked over at him, grinning while the two goats kept rubbing up against him, wanting the bottles of milk she'd been warming in the large bottle warmer she kept in the other room.

"Protocol dictates the more formal name, and I wouldn't want you to think that just because we spent the night together…er, I mean, just because we slept… Yes, Jet will be fine."

She chuckled under her breath at the sheriff's— at Jet's—obvious awkwardness with the situation. It was almost as though he'd never spent the night with a woman before, at least not on a platonic basis. The thought caused her to snicker even more.

"Am I missing something?" he asked, obviously catching her hidden laughter.

"It's the llamas. They keep nipping at my shirt collar." Which they were.

The pen was fairly large, about fifteen by eighteen feet, but it wasn't enough room for them to run and play in, so she was getting all their extra energy. They kept rubbing up against her, then running around in a circle only to do it again. One was chocolate brown, the male, and the other almost pure white, a female.

"They seem kind of aggressive. Shouldn't they be in a barn somewhere, instead of cooped up in that pen?"

Jet was absolutely right, but she'd had no choice. They'd been left on her doorstep at a most inopportune time.

"They're not aggressive, more playful than anything else. Llamas are the sweetest animals you can ever have on a ranch. Plus, they're better protectors against coyotes or hawks or even possums. They only arrived this afternoon or I would have brought them out to my parents' ranch until I could find a home for them. Problem was, I couldn't risk driving all the way out there and getting stuck on my way back, so instead I decided to keep them here for a bit. I should be able to move them out tomorrow or the next day at most."

He gave one of the goats a pat on the head before it danced off, then loved up the other one when it nudged his leg. From all that she'd seen so far that night, Sheriff Jet Wilson was not the brute she had made him out to be. Jet Wilson seemed to be as soft and cuddly underneath that hard outer shell as any of her critters. A fact she would try to remember the next time he fined her for one of her forbidden country animals.

"No worries. Really. I understand."

Now she really didn't understand him, not even remotely. Who was this guy? How could she have misread him so badly?

"Why the change of heart? Why aren't you writing up a ticket? What changed?"

He turned to her and shrugged. "It's not your fault the people of this town have decided to abandon their animals…and now their babies…on your doorstep. I guess I never understood what that meant before. These little guys deserve a break, deserve a new start, and apparently the townsfolk think you can give it to them. You're quite the protector, Doctor…I mean Coco…and everyone seems to know that."

"Does that mean you'll dismiss my pending fines?"

Now that he'd seemed to have a change of heart, she felt hopeful about asking for those dang fines to go away.

He stood up straight and looked directly into her eyes, wearing his official deadpan expression again. As if he could switch that authoritarian look on and off at will. "No," he said with certainty. "It just means I won't give you another fine for this group… That's contingent upon your finding a place for the goats and llamas as soon as the weather clears up. A place outside city limits."

She stuck a fist to her hip, somewhat peeved he couldn't let those fines go, but underneath all her hope, she was beginning to understand his tough position.

"Well, that's something. I guess."

"It's the least I can do seeing as how you've taken in Lily."

She didn't want him getting any ideas about her caring for Lily. Sure, she felt sorry for the poor little thing, and Lily had already made an inroad into Coco's heart, but she couldn't allow herself to spend too much time with the child or she would never want to let her go.

"Just for the night or until the weather clears up and the roads get plowed. With my schedule, I certainly can't take in a baby."

Which was true, so she latched onto that thought and held it close. It would allow her to hand Lily over to the authorities without breaking her heart. The abandoned animals were fine, but an abandoned baby caused her way too much internal grief, a grief she wasn't prepared to spill anytime soon...especially not in front of Jet Wilson. Sure, he had a softer side, but that outer shell was as hard as steel and she had no intention of going up against it.

"Nor are you qualified to take her."

Coco's internal antenna went up. Did he know something about her? Was there gossip going around that she didn't know about? "What's that supposed to mean?"

He stepped out of the goat pen, to the dismay of both goats, slipped off his gloves and headed for the next room that contained a refrigerator, a large bottle warmer and some supplies. "Not what you're thinking," he shouted back. She heard him open the lid on the bottle warmer. "Idaho has rules about who can be a temporary guardian for an abandoned baby, and you aren't certified. I checked."

She relaxed a bit. He'd merely been referring to some law she knew little about.

"And I suppose you are?"

He stepped back into the main room, holding a large bottle of warmed milk in each hand. Large nipples cupped the tops of the bottles.

"By default, yes. But I also had to take a few classes."

The goats bleated at the end of the pen, their heads hanging over the wire mesh, mouths open in anticipation.

"But I thought you said you knew all about caring for a baby from growing up in foster care?"

"I guess it's a combination of both."

He held both bottles down so the kids could nurse. They pulled down the milk as if they'd been starving, which they weren't. She'd fed them in the morning before she'd begun her day, and now before bed. Twice a day was sufficient for these little guys. The good thing about these two was that their owner had at least disbudded them well, so their horns wouldn't grow, a problem for domesticated goats.

"I wish I knew more about caring for babies. I only know animals," Coco told him.

The goats pushed and knocked their bottles, wanting the milk to come out faster, but Coco had given them the appropriate nipple with the appropriate slice in the top for a controlled flow. Anything more and they'd choke.

"It's the same thing. Neither a baby nor an animal can tell you what's wrong. You have to use your intuition and your expertise, and hope that you're right. I mean, look at these little guys. You manage to keep them all healthy, right?"

"Most of the time, but even with them, I can sometimes get it wrong."

"But you strike me as the type of doctor who keeps trying until you do get it right."

"Thanks. I like to think that I do. Yes."

She appreciated his confidence in her. Where he'd gotten it, she didn't know, but she sure liked it. Aside from her brother, Carson, her sisters, Kenzie, Callie and Kayla, her dad and mom, and a handful of the local ranchers, she didn't always get that kind of respect. There were times when she'd get outright skepticism. Not that she minded it, or resented it. She understood. Those animals meant thousands of dollars to the ranchers. Sometimes a healthy animal or a sick animal stood between a rancher and bankruptcy. A vet could, at times, make or break a ranch depending on his or her diagnosis. So it had better be the correct one.

"Have you always wanted to be a vet?"

She nodded. "I think for as long as I could remember. I love my job and I'm blessed that when Doctor Graham retired, he left his practice to me. What about you? Have you always wanted to be a sheriff?"

He chuckled. "Absolutely not. I wanted to be a bus driver, or a truck driver, then a fireman, a cowboy or a rodeo star, and for a short time I wanted to be a rock star. I play a mean guitar."

She smiled, envisioning Jet in tight black leather pants, no shirt and eyeliner. He clearly didn't fit the image. "Then how on earth did you end up being a sheriff?"

"When I got out of the military, I didn't know what to do with myself until I met Sheriff Perkins over in Chubbuck, who was looking for a deputy. The pay was good enough to keep me off the street, and I liked the sheriff, so I applied and got the job. He trained me, and a couple years ago when this job came up, he pushed me out of the nest and gave me a good reference. The rest, as they say, is history."

"So, does that mean you like it?"

"For the most part, it suits me."

"When doesn't it suit you?"

The baby goats emptied their bottles, their tails wagging like mad, indicating that their bellies were nice and full before Jet pulled the bottles away. They fussed for a minute, then went about bumping heads and playing.

He turned to her, looking sullen. "When I have to deal with an abandoned baby."

"That's exactly how I feel when someone abandons an animal on my doorstep. But a baby is a hundred times worse."

"So, it's safe to say, Lily is tough for us both."

"She's breaking my heart in more ways than I want to admit."

"Mine, too," he said, and in that moment, he took her breath away.

THE SNOW HAD crept up above his knees, and he could no longer feel his feet or fingers. Every tree, rock and surface around him was covered in thick, heavy snow that continued to fall in great big lacy flakes, making visibility virtually impossible.

How he'd gotten out on a hillside, he didn't know.

With each breath, a billow of steam surrounded his face. His entire body shook from cold, but Jet couldn't stop moving forward. He knew he had to keep going, keep walking, one foot in front of the other. He had to keep going. Had to get to Doctor Grant's house.

He could barely make out a structure in the distance, a log cabin, blanketed in snow, with smoke swirling up out of the chimney and bright yellow lights glowing from the three windows, beckoning him forward.

In the distance he heard a baby cry, faint at first, then growing louder and louder with each step until the sound pierced his ears. He soon realized that he carried the screaming baby under his coat, held it tight against his chest. But why hadn't he known this before? What was wrong with him? How could he have not been aware? If he had known that the baby was his responsibility, he would have walked faster. He wouldn't have had that drink with the woman in the black lace dress at the bar. Was it her baby?

No. He seemed to know that for a fact.

But where did it come from? Who gave him a baby?

The little darling screamed louder until his ears hurt, until he vibrated from the sound of the baby wrapped in a pink blanket. Then, suddenly, she began to slip from his grasp. He could no longer hold her. His hands were numb. He couldn't feel her, couldn't protect her. She kept slipping away…

"Noooo!" he yelled, jerking awake and immediately realizing it had been a dream—a really bad dream. But the crying had been real, and the cold he'd felt in the dream was also real. His blankets had all fallen on the floor, and his body ached from the weird position he'd been in trying to get comfortable on the mini sofa. When he flexed his fingers on his right hand, a thousand needles shot through his fingers telling him that he'd somehow cut off the circulation.

He sat up, taking in his unfamiliar surroundings. Someone flipped a light switch and his eyes stung for a moment as they adjusted to the bright light.

That's when he heard Punky yapping from somewhere off in the distance.

"Something's wrong with Lily," Coco said as she held Lily in her arms. "I took her temperature and it's one hundred and one. I made a bottle, but she won't take it."

"Did you examine her?"

Punky came running in, stopping at Coco's feet. His barking only adding to the noise factor already coming from Lily's intense wails.

"I was just about to."

Coco seemed levelheaded and cool, despite the squirming baby in her arms and the barking dog at her feet.

"Did you take an anal temperature? That's the only way to tell what's real with a baby this small."

"No, I took it under her arm."

"Let's put her on the table with a couple blankets under her," Jet suggested. He thought that would be the easiest way. "And take that temperature again."

Coco leaned over and spoke to Punky directly. "Stop. It's okay. Lily is okay. Sit."

At once the dog stopped barking and sat obediently on his haunches waiting for another command.

"How'd you do that?" Jet asked, amazed at how quickly the tiny dog obeyed.

"Training. Punky thinks he's a German shepherd and his bark means danger. I'm merely telling him that everything is okay."

"Wow. I wish I could get some ornery people to respond that way."

"It's all in the tone of voice."

"I'll keep that in mind the next time I'm trying to arrest someone."

She grinned. "I'll need a regular-sized stethoscope and an otoscope for her ears. I have small ones down in the clinic." She approached Jet with Lily in her arms. "Can you take her while I get a few things?"

"Sure. Just let me slip on my jeans," Jet told her, then he picked up his pants off the floor and slipped them on over his long tight black cotton underwear, then zipped them up. Normally he might have been a little hesitant about getting dressed in front of a woman he didn't know intimately, but there was something different about Coco, something easygoing about her that kept all his apprehensions at bay.

He wasn't wearing a shirt, which accounted for

the dream of his being so cold—that and he'd been sleeping half-naked without a blanket. No wonder he felt like an icicle. He quickly slipped on his thermal undershirt as well, not bothering with anything else, like his shirt or socks or a belt. Lily needed quick attention, and his needs took a back seat to hers.

He settled Lily in his arms, shushing her as he did, and bouncing her to a rhythm in his head. Her little face was bright red, and her hands were fisted tight, her body tense and her mouth wide-open, screaming with everything she had.

"Hey there, sweet cakes, everything's fine. We're going to fix you right up. I promise. Shhh," he cooed, but Lily wasn't buying any of it and continued on her rampage. Coco returned with what she needed to examine Lily. Punky now paced on the sofa, obviously upset over the turmoil in his house.

"Let me get the blankets," Coco said and within moments she had everything set up on the table.

The first time she went to look inside Lily's ears, Jet noticed that her hands were shaking. "It's okay. You've done this a million times before. Lily isn't any different than any of your other patients. She's a baby in crisis. Take a breath, and slowly let it out. You know how to handle this."

Coco followed his instructions until her breathing became more regular and her hands stopped shaking.

"You're right," she told him with a slight grin. "I'm overreacting to something I know exactly how to do."

Jet held on to Lily, trying to soothe her with a lullaby as Coco listened to her lungs and heart, and checked inside her ears. Then she gently but expertly placed a hand on Lily's forehead, which caused her to cry even harder, if that was even possible.

Since the lullaby was no longer working, Jet rocked out on Michael Jackson's "Beat It." For whatever reason, that seemed to do the trick, along with baby Lily finding her own fist to suck on. Lily had exchanged crying for little slurping noises.

"She has a slight infection in one of her ears, and her temperature is elevated."

"What's our next step?" Jet asked as he slipped a fresh diaper on Lily and zipped up her sleeper gown.

"She's too young for any kind of drug. I think what we need to do is put a warm compress up to her ear and bathe her in tepid water with a cloth to bring down her fever."

"Whatever you think is best."

"I appreciate your confidence in me."

"Anytime," he told her with a nod and a grin, absolutely believing that she knew exactly what to do.

Forty-five minutes later, after working together, both of them singing most of Michael Jackson's hits, and after much screaming and fussing due to the wet cloth both on Lily's ear and on her tiny body, all his faith in Coco had been affirmed.

Lily had calmed down enough to take her bottle, and Jet was finally able to take a deep breath. The crisis had passed.

Now Coco leaned against the headboard on her bed as Lily happily suckled the formula. Her temperature had read ninety-nine the last time Coco had checked, and the inflammation in Lily's ear seemed to be subsiding.

Without giving it much thought, Jet climbed up on the bed beside Coco and leaned back on the headboard as Punky, who had used his little step stool to get up on the bed, curled up in a tight ball between them. As if on cue, he and Jet let out simultaneous loud sighs.

"Punky and I feel about the same," Jet said. "You were amazing, and I'm so glad Lily seems to be feeling better. I don't know what I would've done on my own. My expertise, if you could call it that, is limited to feeding and clothing and general, all-around care. Anything medical is out of my league. Although, I have been known to bring down a few fevers in my day, and I'm great with cuts and scraped knees." Jet crossed his long legs on her bed, slipping his cold bare feet under the mess of blankets and the comforter at the end of the bed.

"Thanks. Your patience and guidance were pretty amazing, too," Coco told him, grinning. "You'll make a great dad someday, if you ever want kids."

They both kept their voices to a calm whisper, cautious that their unfamiliar tones might stir Lily up again.

He turned his head to look at her, now only inches away from her lovely face, taking a second to notice the slope of her delicate nose, her full lips, the tiny laugh lines that seemed to embrace the corners of her mouth and the slight dimple in her right cheek as she stared down at Lily, who eagerly drank from the bottle.

"I do…someday, hopefully, but not while I'm in law enforcement. Too risky. I'm not about to leave my son or daughter without a father. I'd need a safe nine-to-five job first or a ranch to run or a snowplow to drive."

"So you're saying you won't have kids as long as you're the sheriff?"

"I will not."

"But I thought you said this job suits you?"

"It does, but not if I want to raise a family. Cops get killed or badly injured in the line of duty all the time. I won't do that to my child."

"Like your dad did to you? What happened to your parents? Was your dad in law enforcement?"

"He was a hotshot and lost his life fighting fire in Yellowstone."

"I'm so sorry. That must have been awful."

"I don't remember much about it, just that I missed him for a very long time. Still do, sometimes." He could barely remember his dad. All he had were glimpses of him laughing, or smiling down at him, not enough to know anything about the man behind the images.

"And your mom?"

Coco slipped the bottle out of Lily's rosebud mouth, put it down on the bedside table, then placed Lily on her shoulder. She fussed for a bit, but then burped a couple times. Soon Lily once again contentedly suckled her bottle.

Coco was a natural at this mother thing, unlike Jet's own mom, who never really got the hang of it.

"I don't blame my mom. She never had the temperament to raise a child on her own. It was only supposed to be temporary…leaving me in foster care… but weeks turned into months and months turned into years. She took me back when I was almost seventeen, but by then I was so used to being on my own that all we did was fight. We get along now, but the damage had already been done. She lives in Florida with her childhood sweetheart. I hate Florida. Way too hot and muggy for me.

"But I don't want to talk about me anymore. You're a natural at this, the way you handle Lily, the way you handled the emergency tonight. You'd make a great mom. I'm surprised you don't already have a houseful of babies. Watching you with Lily, and the love you show to all your critters, any child would be lucky to have you as their mom."

He'd meant it as a compliment, not as an affront, but all of a sudden, Coco's eyes watered and big tears slipped down her beautiful cheeks. "No. What's wrong? Did I say something to offend you? I'm sorry if I did. Things come out of my mouth sometimes that I don't take time to think through. I didn't mean anything negative. Honest."

She wiped the tears away with her hand. "You didn't know. How could you? No one really knows, not even my family."

"Is it something you want to talk about? Because I'm like a priest in a confessional. Whatever you tell me is locked away…unless it's something illegal. Then don't tell me or I'll have to haul you off to jail, and I really wouldn't like that considering everything we just went through to get Lily to stop crying. And besides, the weather sucks."

He got her to smile again and his world lit up. "It's nothing illegal."

"Good, then what is it?"

She turned to look at him, her face streaked with tears. "Last year, I was diagnosed with moderate to severe endometrioses. It's when tissue that lines the inside of a woman's uterus grows outside the uterus. When it attacks the ovaries, cysts form. I have both of those issues and the chances of my getting pregnant without surgery or in vitro fertilization go down significantly with each passing year. That's why I wanted you to simply take Lily. I didn't want to be around her to remind me, and I certainly didn't want to give her my heart."

He couldn't help himself. He reached over and ran his finger down her cheek. "From looking at you now, both of those things have happened."

She gazed down at Lily, smiling and pulling her in tighter. She had fallen asleep, so Coco gently removed the nipple from her little mouth. Lily sighed and stretched, but never opened her eyes. Instead, she merely turned her head sideways, as if she was about to nurse on Coco's breast, and fell into a deep, comfortable sleep.

"Any man you marry will certainly love you enough to understand, and help you through any kind of surgery or procedure you want to do in order to get pregnant. And if that's not an option, then the two of you can adopt a baby just like Lily."

"I doubt there's another baby in the entire world like Lily. Look at how sweet she is, that little cherub face, and her deep blue eyes, and the way she seems to be smiling whenever she's content. And the way she coos when you talk to her, like she's trying to answer you. I tried so hard to keep my emotions out of this, but when Lily woke up with a fever under my watch, I couldn't help but fall in love with her. I know she has to leave me in the morning, and it's ripping me apart."

"You want to know something?"

She nodded.

"Giving her up is ripping me apart, as well."

Then, wanting to protect both Lily and Coco, he reached out and Coco scooted into his embrace, bringing sleeping Lily along with her. When they were both nestled in tight, with Coco's head leaning on his shoulder, a strong wave of compassion washed over him, causing his own eyes to well up with emotion. He could only imagine the grief Coco was feeling holding that tiny baby in her arms.

She continued, "I know I shouldn't question it, but I can't even begin to imagine what could have drove Lily's mother to leave her child with strangers. The thought is inconceivable to me. I only wish I could talk to Lily's mom, meet her, get to know her reasons and maybe try to convince her to reconsider, but I know it's not my place to do any of those things. Still, I can't help but wonder if she's missing her baby on this cold snowy night, or if she's relieved she finally got rid of her. Either way, it breaks my heart."

He couldn't help but kiss her on her forehead, stroke her hair and pull her in tighter. In all his adult life, he'd never felt closer to a woman than he had just then.

He knew she was involved with Russ Knightly, a man he wouldn't drive across town to meet, and from what he saw earlier that night, Coco was probably in love with him, although Jet couldn't for the life of him understand why. Still, he knew he and Coco had shared something meaningful, and no matter what happened between them in the days to come, he'd always feel close to her.

He wanted to confess his own heartbreak about Lily's abandonment and about having to hand her over to strangers who would only be her caretakers and nothing more, but he changed his mind. In comforting Coco, he also comforted himself, and for now, that was all he needed. All that mattered.

Tomorrow, everything would be different, and for all they knew, Lily's mom might return, looking for her precious baby.

Chapter Four

Coco awoke slowly, wrapped up in Russ's arms, content as a kitten in the sun, only there was no sun, only a sort of darkness that a snowy sky can bring, and when she gazed up at her man, it wasn't Russ, but Sheriff Jet Wilson, sound asleep.

Punky stretched his front legs out, shook off sleep and jumped off the bed, waiting for her to let him out on the upstairs patio. He had a little area on the patio where he went and did his business when she couldn't take him out for a walk. This was one of those moments.

She quickly but ever so carefully slid out of Jet's embrace and panicked over the whereabouts of baby Lily. The last thing she remembered was holding Lily as she fell asleep in Coco's arms, while she fell asleep in Jet's arms.

"Oh, no," she whispered to herself. When she slid out of bed, she nearly hit her shin on an open drawer, and before she could scold herself for being so absent-minded, she noticed that baby Lily lay all snuggled up on her back, sound asleep inside the drawer that had been lined with soft blankets.

Coco was ever so tempted to pick her up and hold her tight, but she stopped short as she fully realized that she'd spent the night in the same bed as Jet Wilson, wrapped in his arms.

She tried to remember if anything sexual took place during the night, but when her mind came up clean, she let out a thankful sigh. Although, looking at him now, his hair all messed up, the pillow scrunched under his head and that fabulous big muscled body taking up space on her bed, she wasn't sure if she would've minded if something sexual had taken place…at least a kiss or two.

She scolded herself for thinking such reckless thoughts as she led Punky through the kitchen, then opened the back door for him to go out. A blast of icy wind nearly froze her solid as she waited in the slightly open doorway. Snow blew in on her and covered her back patio in great big drifts that seemed higher than she was tall. Punky took two steps out the door and did his duty right there on the disposable mat, not wanting to go any farther. She always kept a thick paper mat close by for Punky in case of bad weather, and this ranked as some of the worst.

"I don't blame you, Punky," she told him as he came running back into the warmth of the kitchen.

When she headed back to the bedroom she reminded herself that she already had a boyfriend… kind of. Okay, so she and Russ hadn't slept together yet, but that was merely a matter of poor timing, she felt sure of it. She'd been in love with Russ for years now, albeit one-sided, but nevertheless, she cared for him. He was everything she'd ever wanted…aside from the fact that he didn't seem to like children… but then she couldn't have children, at least, not very easily.

She had wanted to assume that the man she would marry would love her enough to want to go through all the steps needed for her to carry their own baby, or that perhaps he would even consider adopting.

Maybe the assumption wasn't a fair one.

She hadn't been all that honest with Russ about her pregnancy issues really, insofar as she hadn't told him everything that she'd said to Jet last night.

And why she'd confided in Jet was beyond her. She'd kept that secret to herself for over a year now, and yet, there she was, blabbing like a schoolgirl.

Still scolding herself, she quickly showered, got dressed and added more makeup than she usually wore on a daily basis, telling herself that she wanted to look good if and when Russ stopped by. She also admitted that she wanted to look good for Jet, as well.

Oh, this was getting complicated and she didn't fully understand why. Russ was her man, not Jet Wilson, who couldn't even fully embrace being a sheriff. At least Russ knew exactly what career and future he wanted, and was willing to work really hard to get there. It sounded as if Jet had hardly worked at all to get his job; it was more or less handed to him.

While Jet and Lily both slept, she and Punky ambled downstairs to take care of the animals. Punky liked to check on the goats, and they liked to try to catch him. Punky believed he was a brute of a big dog, so nothing scared him, not even when the goats tried to butt him with their heads.

When the cages were cleaned and the goats, piglet, llamas, kittens and one lonely puppy were fed, along with the tortoise, Coco and Punky went back upstairs only to find Jet pouring batter onto her waffle iron, while baby Lily squirmed and cooed in her bassinet on the kitchen counter.

"Morning," Sheriff Jet Wilson said, a lilt in his voice that she'd never heard before.

"Good morning. Not only can you take care of an infant, but you can cook, as well?"

"Nothing too fancy, but yes. I make a mean waffle. How do you like your bacon?"

"Dry, just like my eggs, but let me help. What can I do?"

"You can play with Lily, who drank her entire bottle, I might add. She seems to be feeling better this morning, all thanks to you."

Coco went over and peeked in at Lily, who stared up at the ceiling lights, her little legs flexing and her tiny fingers spread out on her chest. A bright red streak crossed her right cheek.

"Aw, looks like her nails need clipping."

"Already taken care of."

Coco could hardly believe this guy. "Is there anything you can't do?"

His entire face lit up with a wide grin. "Several things."

"Name a few."

She went over to the stove and felt the kettle, already hot, so she made a cup of English Breakfast using a tea bag from her plentiful stash of teas.

"I can't ride a horse very well. Never really learned."

"I can teach you," she said without really thinking about what that meant. "We're all great riders in my family."

"If you live in Briggs, you know all about the riding skills of the Grant family. Seen your brother compete out at the fairgrounds, and your sisters Callie and Kenzie are expert riders."

She didn't want to brag, but… "I can rope a steer while on horseback faster than any of 'em. Just haven't done it in a while. You'd give me a reason to get back in the saddle, so to speak."

"I may take you up on that," he said as he plated their food. "One slice of bacon or two?"

"Three, if you made enough."

It was the first time in her entire adult life that a man other than her father or brother had made breakfast for her.

"I made plenty."

He piled her plate with scrambled eggs, a waffle and three slices of bacon. It looked yummy and she couldn't wait to dig in.

"Anything else you're not good at?"

"Are we still on me? How about you? I've seen you with Lily, and all your critters downstairs. You're amazing. And now you tell me you can rope a steer while on horseback. What can't you do?"

"Relationships."

He shook his head. "I can't believe that. You must have guys beating down your door."

Everything was cooked to perfection, the waffle crispy on the outside and light as air on the inside, the bacon dry and the eggs perfectly perfect.

"Just one guy at the moment, and after last night, I don't know if he'll come knocking anytime soon."

His eyebrow crooked up slightly, as if he was skeptical about something.

"He'll be back. I guarantee it. He's not going to let one little baby stand in his way. He strikes me as the kind of guy who always gets what he wants."

"Do I detect a little jealousy in that statement? I mean, isn't that good for someone who wants to be mayor?"

"Depends on who he has to step on to get there."

"So far, to my knowledge, he hasn't stepped on anyone."

"He may be good at hiding the bodies."

She detected more than jealousy. She detected a disdain for Russ, her knight in shining armor. "You don't like him very much, do you?"

He topped off his coffee, then added cream and a teaspoon of sugar. She couldn't remember the last time she saw anyone add real sugar to their beverage. The only reason she kept it around was occasionally she liked to bake something, but that hadn't happened in months.

"Can't say that I do."

"Why not?"

He hesitated, as if deciding how honest he wanted

to be with his feelings. "My own personal reasons, but hey, if he's your man, then who am I to rain on your parade."

"I didn't know I was in a parade."

"Dating a prominent figure like Russ Knightly— every time you and he go out that door, you probably get a following."

She knew he was right, but still. "Sometimes, but maybe I like it."

"Don't you know?"

She hated that he tripped her up. "No. I mean yes. I mean, that's only temporary. Once he's elected, things will quiet down."

"He doesn't strike me as the kind of guy who does anything in a quiet fashion."

She suddenly didn't like where this conversation was going. "Okay. Enough about me and my relation-ship, which you obviously don't approve of. What about you and your relationships? I suppose you have women lining up at the jailhouse just dying for your attention?"

"If they are, I haven't noticed."

She liked how he suddenly tried to be coy... As if.

"Are you secretly dating anyone?"

"Why would it be a secret?"

She shrugged. "You strike me as a private sort of guy."

"I am, but not that private. I just keep picking the wrong kind of girl."

"And what kind is that?"

"The kind who can't seem to date one guy at a time."

"You mean like Dani Century?"

"How'd you know about her?"

"It's a small town."

Everyone knew he'd dated Dani, and that she dumped him for a rodeo rat.

"She said she wanted a steady guy and that she wanted to put down roots."

"You should've asked her how deep. That girl wasn't about to stick around long enough to break through the topsoil."

Jet chuckled softly as he took a bite of his eggs. "Don't I know it. You have a way with words. Anybody ever tell you that?"

"You're the first, but thanks."

She took the last bite of her waffle, which was now swimming in maple syrup.

"How about another waffle? I still have enough batter for one more."

"Sure," she told him, wanting their breakfast to last a little longer. "Your waffles are amazing, crispy but light as a feather."

"Sally Crane's recipe, foster family number five when I was about ten. She got it from her mom who came from Sweden."

"But how did you learn it? Seems a little odd for a ten year old to want to know how to make a waffle."

"That's 'cause I was an odd kid. Whenever I liked something, whether it was something to eat, or build, or a skill I thought would be good to know, I watched the person carefully and wrote everything down in a journal. Then I'd memorize it, because keeping any kind of personal possessions in foster care wasn't always possible."

"That explains a lot about your ability to handle Lily. What a crafty kid you must have been."

"You could say that, but to me, it was more about survival. The more I knew, the more I thought adults would want to keep me around. But that didn't pan out the way I thought it would."

"I can't imagine how tough and confusing it must have been for you, or for that matter, for all the children who are in foster care. I'm so worried about Lily, and what her future will be like."

He gazed at her, warmth and concern all over his face. "Maybe her mom will come back for her. I hope that's the case, but if she doesn't, Lily has a good chance of getting adopted fairly quickly. Babies and toddlers have the best chance of settling into a permanent home. It's the children five and over who have a harder time of it."

"My siblings and I are blessed. You and Lily have made that abundantly clear. I'll never take my childhood for granted again."

"Now, how about that second waffle?" he asked, while opening the lid on the waffle iron, steam pouring out.

Coco held up her plate. "Yes, please, and more of that great bacon, as well."

Jet filled her plate and she immediately poured on more syrup and took a big bite. She couldn't remember when she'd been so honest with a guy, and he'd been so honest with her. She held back with Russ, just as she was sure he did the same with her. But that would all change once they were a true couple.

As they sat there, sharing breakfast, listening to Lily's contented coos, she couldn't help the many thoughts that flitted through her mind on what it would be like to be married to Sheriff Jet Wilson. Not only had he cooked her a perfect breakfast, with perfectly crispy waffles, crispy bacon and soft scrambled eggs, but he'd showered, shaved with one of her plastic razors, no doubt, and gotten completely dressed in the jeans and long-sleeved dark-gray shirt he'd worn the previous night. She'd never noticed how good he looked in civilian clothes, but she sure did now.

Her mind wandered a bit, recalling how warm and safe she'd felt last night, resting her head on his shoulder, cuddling up against his strong chest, as he now talked about what the day might be like for him and who he needed to call first about baby Lily.

It was at that moment that her cell phone rang. The distinctive tune told her Russ, the man of her dreams, the man she wanted to spend the rest of her life with, the man she should have been sharing breakfast with this morning, was on the line.

But for some inexplicable reason, she didn't have those feelings exactly.

"Someone you're avoiding?" Jet asked as the tune played on and on.

She wished she'd switched her phone to vibrate.

"No. Of course not. Had to swallow my last bite first."

Jet stood when the bell went off on the waffle iron indicating that the next waffle was cooked, and he slipped it out onto a clean plate while she took the call…walking away from the table and into the living room for some privacy.

"Hey, Russ," she said into the phone, trying to sound excited.

"Hey, yourself. I take it that arrogant sheriff and the screaming baby are gone by now?"

"Um, sure," she said, flat-out lying. This was one time when she couldn't bear to tell Russ the truth. Besides, the sheriff and Lily would be gone for good once breakfast was over. She was sure of it.

"Unless you're walking, nobody's going anywhere," Drew Gillian told Jet as she stood in the kitchen drinking a supersize cup of coffee. "Even though I live down the street, getting here on foot wasn't easy, and driving anywhere would be next to impossible." Drew couldn't have been more than nineteen or twenty years old, had shoulder-length blond hair with purple steaks, a classic Roman nose, almond-shaped amber-colored eyes, cherub-formed lips with a beauty mark right above her top lip and a petite five-foot-two figure. Personality wise, she reminded Jet of Punky, a tiny bundle of roar.

"That's impossible," Jet countered, then took off down the stairs to check it out for himself. He'd looked out the window earlier that morning, before he'd sat down for breakfast, and he'd checked the weather report. Both had indicated that the city was coming back to life.

He opened the front door.

More snow had fallen in that hour or so he'd taken to enjoy breakfast, and it was still falling now. "Come on!"

His phone chirped in his pocket, and when he looked at the screen, he saw the deputy sheriff's smiling face from a picture he'd taken during the summer's Western Days festival. Nash had replaced Deputy Sheriff Hunter Sears, who'd gotten married and moved to Oregon soon thereafter.

"What's up?" Jet said into the phone after he accepted the call.

"A lot," Nash Young said. "Got several people stranded in their cars, a couple roofs collapsed, one on a business in town, but thankfully nobody was hurt, and what appears to be a break-in overnight at a house in the two hundred block of Main Street. Nothing is reported missing, though. I think whoever it was only wanted to get in out of the cold. Oh, yeah, and someone left you a note at the jail."

"Did you see who it was?"

"No. It was under the door when I opened up this morning. Where'd you get stranded last night? Looks like you left this place in a hurry. Your half-eaten dinner is still on your desk."

"Long story. An abandoned baby named Lily. I'm over here at Doctor Grant's clinic."

"A real baby? Not a foal or a calf or a puppy, but an actual human baby?"

"Yep, a two-week-old girl named Lily, according to the note."

"Well, in all this snow, I hope Doctor Grant can take care of Lily for a few days, 'cause there's no way you can drive her over to Idaho Falls to Child Protective Services, and from what I heard, the hospital is overrun with everything from a couple heart attacks to some nasty frostbite cases. This kind of weather brings out the worst."

"Thanks for the heads-up."

"You coming in today?"

"Not unless you drive over and pick me up. My rig is snowed in solid."

"Be there as soon as I can," Nash said, then Jet disconnected.

Nash Young's personal truck could get through anything. The tires alone were the size of a small person, and it was fitted with a supercharged engine good enough for any top-fueled drag race. Nothing could stop that vehicle, not even another car, which it could simply drive over. Deputy Sheriff Nash Young drove it for most of the winter months only because he'd designed it after the trucks he'd driven in Monster Jams across the country. He only gave up competing last year when he narrowly escaped an exploding rig and promised his mom he'd do so. Jet had a feeling that it was only a matter of time until he was competing again, but until that happened, Briggs was lucky to have Nash and his four-wheel monster truck to help evacuate stranded motorists almost anywhere across the valley.

When Jet walked back into the kitchen, Drew busied herself playing with Lily and asking way too many questions, questions that sounded more on the nosey, gossipy side rather than the friendly, getting-to-know-Lily side.

"So, Lily's name was written on the back of a receipt from Sammy's Smokehouse?" Drew asked Coco. "That's mighty curious."

"Yeah, and when I first took Lily out of her bassinet, she smelled of barbecue," Coco said.

"You told me about the receipt, but you never told me she smelled of barbecue. Why didn't you tell me this before?" Jet asked, miffed.

"I didn't think it was important."

"It's real important," Drew alleged. "This means whoever had Lily, probably the mom, ate at Sammy's right before she dumped Lily on your front porch. The curious element in all of this is why didn't this distressed mom leave her at the jail? Unless she knew how you take in strays, which would make the mom a resident of Briggs. Only a resident would know about your stray policy."

"For one thing, a baby is hardly a stray," Jet countered, then he turned to Coco. "You have a stray policy? And here I thought these folks left their animals on your doorstep because of convenience. The nearest pound is thirty miles away. If you have an actual policy for strays and didn't register it with the sheriff's department, your fines could be doubled."

"You would do that?"

"It's the law," Jet told her, expecting her to understand…although, from the acerbic look on her face, he didn't think that was the case.

"Fine. You just keep doing what you have to do or how else could you possibly sleep at night?"

"I don't, remember?"

"That's not what I saw last night."

"Sheriff Wilson spent the night?" Drew asked with a teasing grin.

"That's none of your business," both Coco and Jet said in unison.

Drew held up a hand. "Chill, I won't tell anyone."

"Jet didn't have anywhere else to go. The snow was too deep."

"Jet?" Drew asked. "You call the sheriff Jet?"

Jet stepped in front of Coco, facing Drew. He'd caught the look of anger on Coco's face and decided he needed to de-escalate this situation before she admitted that she and Jet had slept in the same bed together.

"Here's what happened, not that it's anybody's business, but just to get the record straight. Baby Lily was left on Doctor Grant's doorstep sometime right before ten last night. Soon thereafter, the doctor phoned me about an abandoned baby, and after stopping at Whipple's for supplies, I arrived to take the child. By the time we had her changed and fed, the snow inhibited me from leaving, so I spent the entire night on the sofa while Doctor Grant and Lily slept in her bed.

"As far as the mom or whoever left the baby on Doctor Grant's doorstep rather than mine goes, I can only speculate that Sammy's is on this side of town, and with all the snow that fell last night, driving any farther was next to impossible. And besides, I didn't get back to the jail until after ten thirty."

"Where were you?" Drew asked like she was trying to solve a mystery.

"On official business."

"No, you weren't. You were ahead of me in line at the pickup window at Sammy's."

Jet suddenly hated living in a small town.

Normally, Jet ate at Sammy's three times a week, and he always ate inside. He'd been worried about the snow buildup last night, so he'd decided on takeout instead. He wondered if he'd eaten inside the restaurant last night, would he have seen the mom or whoever had Lily? Things might be a lot different right now if he had…especially given the third degree by Drew Gillian.

"Look, we can't speculate on who left Lily or why. That's not our concern. All we can do now is keep her fed and safe until I can drive her over to Child Protective Services in Idaho Falls so the right people can take care of her. Thus far there's nothing coming in about a stolen baby, or a missing baby. The woman I spoke to is waiting for her, and will handle the case."

Drew shook her head. "Then she'll be a ward of the state?"

"Something like that, yes." He turned to Coco. "Deputy Sheriff Nash Young will be by soon to pick me up. Do you think you can take care of Lily until later today? By then, the roads should be open and I can drive her over. You're free to join me if you want to."

"Thanks, but I can't."

"I know how you feel about Lily, and this is tough for both of us, but it's something we have to do. It might make you feel better if you can see where she'll be going."

Her face darkened, and Jet suspected something else troubled Coco other than just giving up Lily.

"Jet, it's not that I don't want to go with you… It's that…I have a date with Russ tonight."

Jet quickly took a step back, feeling as if she'd just slapped him. He should've realized that call from Russ earlier meant more than just a friendly good-morning greeting. "Oh, but I thought… Yes. Of course you do. Why wouldn't you? I simply assumed… But you know what they say about anyone who assumes. Anyway, I'll be going. I'll call you before I stop by to pick up Lily. By then I should have a car seat, as well. Okay, I guess I'll be heading out."

"Jet, I…"

"No. My mistake. We're good. All good." A horn sounded from outside, signaling that Nash had arrived. Jet faced Drew. "For Lily's sake, it might be best if you kept all this to yourself."

"Whatever you say, Sheriff," Drew told him, her phone only inches away from her arm as she sat in a kitchen chair with Lily resting on a soft pillow positioned carefully on Drew's lap.

Jet knew that gossip about Lily and most likely about his spending the night at the doctor's apartment would be all over town before Jet drove away from the front door.

He'd wager Drew's fingers were itching to start texting.

INFANT SUPPLIES STARTED coming in almost before Coco knew what was happening, and soon it looked like a baby shower had exploded inside her once modest single woman's apartment. Gone were the assortment of scented candles and silk throw pillows, and in their place were tiny coats, chew toys, boxes of diapers, blankets of all sizes and colors, onesies, tiny dresses, tights, itty-bitty shoes, handmade knit sweaters, caps and even mittens. A variety of bottles lined her kitchen counters, along with electric bottle warmers, blenders, plastic baby dishes and tiny spoons. There wasn't one flat surface that didn't have some sort of baby item on it, not one flat surface that even slightly resembled what was once her apartment, her home.

Now it was all about Lily, and no amount of reasoning could sway the good folks of Briggs, Idaho, not to contribute to this tiny abandoned baby. They made the trek through the heavy snow on snowshoes, by sled and by sheer willpower. Even when Coco would try to tell them that Sheriff Wilson would be taking Lily to Child Protective Services later that evening, no one seemed to listen. Even her sister-in-law, Zoe, had made the journey over to bring cloth diapers, which she explained had a myriad of uses. Kenzie was stuck on the ranch, so she couldn't stop by, and Kayla and Callie were snowed in on the other end of town…which was fine by Coco. All this fuss over a baby she couldn't keep seemed a bit silly.

But people just kept bringing gifts over. Mostly items that their babies had grown out of, but there was the occasional new item in the mix, as well.

"Really, Mrs. Walker, these blankets are lovely, but I already have several. You can bring them back to Hess's Department Store and get a refund," Coco told her, but Mrs. Walker, wife to Mr. Walker, who owned Sole Man Shoe Repair, wouldn't hear of it.

"You can never have too many blankets. Go on and keep them," she said as she gazed over at a sleeping Lily all tucked into her bassinet that now sat on the sofa. "Poor darling. Her mom was probably passing through. Sammy has a couple of big signs out on the main road. I bet that's why her mom stopped."

"But how did she know to leave little Lily on Doc Grant's doorstep?" Kendra Myers asked. Kendra, a petite woman with long black hair and a ready smile, had six kids of her own, but still managed to work a couple shifts at Belly Up each week. She'd contributed more of the bottles that Lily liked, along with a cradle and several packages of baby wipes, which Coco truly appreciated considering she went through them like sand slipping through an hourglass.

"That's the puzzler," Amanda Gump said. Not only had Amanda brought over the infant car seat, but she'd brought an assortment of scones, muffins and cookies, as well as an entire chocolate cake from her bakery, Holy Rollers. "She either still lives in Briggs, or she used to live here. Beyond that, I can't imagine who it can be."

"Me, neither," Kitty Sullivan added. She had contributed onesies made of organic cotton, along with a couple of organic cotton receiving blankets. Everyone knew that Kitty Sullivan was into everything organic and wouldn't even consider anything artificial getting anywhere close to her. Last year she'd opened up her own organic shop, The Green Scene, which carried a bit of everything that had an organic source. "All the pregnant women I know are still pregnant."

"I wish we could figure this out," Cindy Whipple said. "When the sheriff stopped by last night, he was being very tight-lipped about the whole thing."

"That's because Idaho has laws to guard the identity of the mother and protect her during the first thirty days," Coco warned, wanting everyone to leave now. "She has the right to full anonymity, and there's nothing we can do about it."

"Maybe so," Cindy said, "but wouldn't you like to know?"

"No," Coco told her. "It's the law."

"Oh, you sound just like Sheriff Wilson," Drew said, dismissing Coco, then going about speculating with the other women as they sat around Coco's dining room table, sipping on coffee and tea while enjoying the assortment of baked goods Amanda had contributed.

But for the first time since Coco had met the sheriff, she appreciated what his strict adherence to the law was all about and felt very protective of Lily's mom, whoever she might be.

"And speaking of the sheriff, Drew says he spent the night," Cindy said, just after she took another sip of tea.

"Did she happen to mention he slept on the sofa? He was trapped here because of the snow. Nothing we could do about it," Coco said.

Coco flashed on the warmth she'd felt cuddled up in Jet's arms, but that was no one's business.

"A good-looking man like that, and you let him sleep on the sofa?" Kendra chided.

"You all know I'm dating Russ Knightly," Coco told them.

"Does Russ know Sheriff Wilson spent the night?" Amanda asked. "'Cause snow or no snow, my Milo would be pacing the floor."

"Nothing happened," Coco said, knowing full well that was the honest truth.

"Well, why not?" Kendra asked, sounding put out. "You're not married…yet. And from what I hear, Russ ain't no saint."

Coco took offense. She knew that Russ had been out with a number of women, but all that had changed once they'd started dating…at least, that was the impression she had. "That's not… He… I…"

Kendra shrugged. "All I'm saying is keep your options open…at least until there's a ring on your finger… if that's something you really want."

"Is Russ going to propose?" Cindy Whipple asked, almost choking on her tea. "Who told you that?"

Then everyone started to speculate about Coco's pending engagement to Russ Knightly even before the search for baby Lily's mom had been settled. All Coco could do was sigh, while she hoped that Jet was having a better day than she was. Rescuing stranded motorists seemed like a much more useful way to spend the afternoon than gossiping about Coco's non-existent love life…in front of her, no less.

Chapter Five

It had been a long, arduous day for both Sheriff Jet Wilson and Deputy Sheriff Nash Young. Not only had they dug out five cars and two pickups, but they'd helped the fire department rescue the entire senior center when the center lost their electricity from a downed power line due to the storm. He and Nash were able to use a couple generators to keep the heat going for the more immobile residents, but most everyone else had to be evacuated to St. Paul's church hall until that line was repaired. Needless to say, getting all those seniors comfortable on cots and folding chairs proved to be a real project.

Fortunately, Father Beau, along with several volunteer parishioners, were real lifesavers, distracting everyone with songs and games and hot liquids. Father Beau deserved a medal of some kind.

Then when the electricity was restored in the center, everyone had to be transported back, which was helped out by Travis Granger and his sled pulled by his two magnificent Clydesdales.

All in all, it was one heck of a day, and it wasn't

over yet. They both had to remain ready to act if there were more needed rescues that night, so Nash would try to get some shut-eye at the jail while Jet took care of Lily. At least, that was the plan. Jet made an appointment to meet with a Marsha Oberlin at eight o'clock in Idaho Falls. She'd agreed to be available whenever he was ready to drop off Lily, but on a night like this, everything could change in a heartbeat.

Both men stomped the caked snow off their boots right outside the front door of the station, then shrugged out of their coats and hung them on the coatrack next to the door. They each took their hats with them to their desks.

"Are you really going to make that hour's drive to Idaho Falls with Lily?" Nash asked once he sat in his wooden swivel chair and leaned back, the chair squeaking with his weight.

Nash's desk was located right outside Jet's office, and unless Jet shut his door, Nash could look right in, which he did. Normally, Nash was an easygoing guy, who stayed out of Jet's business and took to police work like a fish to water. Nash was young and had a backbone, which Jet appreciated a lot. He wore his brown hair extra short, his uniform pressed and his outlook positive.

"I don't have a choice. I can't impose on Doctor Grant for another night, and I certainly can't bring Lily here."

"Why not? You seem to like it here. Oh, there's that letter for you. It's on your desk."

But Jet didn't care about a letter, which was probably someone asking for some kind of favor. Right now, he was defending his logic concerning baby Lily and Doctor Grant.

"I don't like sleeping here, but for right now, with the water problems going on in my apartment building, it's been fine. But this is no place for a baby. There's no telling what can happen."

"This is Briggs, Idaho. Nothing ever happens."

Nash had a point. They ran a small Sheriff's department, one sheriff, one deputy and an answering service. There was one jail cell that so far had only held a handful of perps since Jet came to work there. One of them was Cindy Whipple's husband sleeping off a night of binge drinking. Another perp was a friend of Russ Knightly's, but he'd been in and out so quickly he'd hardly spent any time at all inside that jail cell.

"There's always a first time for everything. I don't want that first time to happen while there's a baby around. It's not safe."

"Want me to drive you? From what I hear, the roads still have some ice."

Jet could go a few miles in Nash's monster truck, but after that, the suspension bounced him around too much. Plus, all that bouncing wasn't safe for a fragile infant. "Thanks, but the SUV will be fine. I'll stop off and pick up a car seat somewhere first."

"Not much open, and besides, I understand that half the town stopped by Doctor Grant's place today with baby stuff. Somebody may have already donated a car seat."

Jet leaned on his desk and stared at Nash. "How do you always know everything that's going on and I don't?"

"I'm Facebook friends with Drew Gillian and she…"

"You can stop right there. I just met Drew this morning and I can tell she likes to keep everyone informed."

Nash smirked. "There's some stuff on there about you spending the night at Doctor Grant's. Now, if I didn't know you better, I'd say Russ Knightly might have a run for his money."

Jet instantly felt a pang of irritation that Drew had spread gossip about himself and the doctor, even though he'd known she would. Still, was there nothing sacred? No friendship that outweighed gossip?

Apparently not in Briggs.

"Nothing happened. I was stuck there because of the snow."

"Convenient, ain't it? I was stuck at Drew's house."

Somehow Jet didn't think that encounter had turned out the same as his. "How'd that go?"

"I was a complete gentleman. Besides, she lives with her parents, and her dad is about six foot four and probably weighs in at well over two hundred and sixty pounds. Believe me, I slept on the sofa. Where'd you sleep?"

"On the sofa," Jet said, but he wasn't very convincing.

"Huh, maybe I needed to send Brick Gillian over… that's his name, Brick, because he's as solid as a brick."

"Both the doctor and I are adults."

"Legally, so are Drew and I, but in Brick's mind, no one shares a bed unless they're married."

"I'll keep that in mind next time I'm snowbound over at Doctor Grant's."

Nash grinned. "Ha! Then you admit that you—"

Jet stood. "I don't admit anything. You're jumping to conclusions that can damage her reputation. She's in a relationship with Russ Knightly, soon to be our new mayor if he has anything to say about it, and come to think of it, they have a date tonight, so I better get going."

Jet had forgotten all about their date. He'd promised to be at Coco's apartment in plenty of time, and he was already running late for both her date and dropping off Lily.

"I won't tell anybody if you admit the truth."

"Nothing happened, and even if it did, which it did not, it's nobody's business."

"Tell that to Russ Knightly. I hear he's the jealous type."

Jet thought about Russ's likely lip-lock with that blonde bombshell over in Jackson Hole. "Maybe so, but he's got nothing to be jealous about between me and his girl, Coco."

"On a first-name basis, huh?"

"I'm going." He secured his hat on his head, grabbed his down parka off the hook and quickly slipped it on.

"Wait!" Nash said from behind Jet. "You forgot the letter."

"What letter?" Jet asked, turning as he opened the

front door. An icy wind slammed against his body, causing him to instantly shiver with its force.

"The one I told you about earlier. The one I found shoved under the door this morning when I came in." Nash hustled over to Jet's desk, retrieved the letter, walked it over and held it out for Jet. As soon as Jet looked at it, he recognized the scratchy writing on the front: *Dani Century*. What could she want?

ASIDE FROM ALL the fuss that afternoon over baby Lily, it had been a relatively calm day for Doctor Grant. No emergency out on a ranch was too dire that she couldn't handle it over the phone, and nothing required her to have to consider driving anywhere to take care of an injured animal. She was grateful for that much.

Besides, she'd liked spending the day with Lily, surrounded with people who wanted to do well by her. Despite the speculation, and the gossip, the residents of Briggs had big hearts, as made apparent by all the clothes, toys and baby supplies scattered around her apartment.

All her orphaned animals had been fed, and their cages cleaned out, thanks to Drew's help. Coco had treated two dogs with bladder infections, prescribed medication for ear mites for three house cats and given yearly booster shots to two golden retrievers whose owners were determined to keep their pets on schedule, despite the weather. Coco didn't know what she would do without Drew to lean on. Drew had somehow managed to keep Coco's patients happy regardless of all the baby chaos.

Once again Coco had slipped into a provocative cocktail dress. This time she wore red lace with three-inch red velvet heels. Not quite as sexy as the previous night's ensemble, but it still clung to all the right places. She and Russ would be attending a dinner and dancing gala for all the business owners in Briggs, at Pauline's Inn on the edge of town. The roads were now somewhat cleared, so there shouldn't be a problem for the partygoers. A car would pick Coco up at eight, and whisk her and Russ to the event, and they would finish what they'd started the previous night. She'd worn her finest black lingerie for the occasion, and intended to end the evening with the sexy love affair they had begun the previous night, only this time, it would be at Russ's estate.

The problem was, she couldn't get Jet Wilson out of her head. Everything about him sent her heart racing and her skin tingling. He'd made her feel safe and relaxed, as if no matter what happened around her, he would handle it. He'd amazed her with his tenderness for Lily, and how adept he was with fulfilling all her needs. And even when Lily awoke in the middle of the night, he didn't shy away. Instead he was right there helping to make sure that whatever was bothering her could be resolved.

The man was simply too surprising to ignore.

Plus, the fact that she was giving up Lily really put a damper on her emotions. Getting out with Russ to a fancy event could only help put her in a better mood…but so far, she wasn't feeling it.

"You're kidding, right?" Drew said as she held Lily on her shoulder and walked her around the room with Punky following close behind, making sure the area was clear of any possible danger. Lily had been fussy while Coco was getting dressed, so she'd asked Drew for some help, which she seemed more than happy to give. "You're going out with Russ tonight? All of this—" she nodded her head and gave Coco the once-over "—is for Russ Knightly?"

Coco stood next to the dining room table, folding baby clothes into a pile, then placing them into a large paper bag with handles.

"He's the man that I'm dating, so yes, it's for Russ."

"And here I thought it was for the sheriff. Don't you like Sheriff Wilson?"

"He's bullheaded and a stickler for the law."

Drew rolled her big doe eyes, thick dark lashes only adding to the exaggerated reaction. "Um, duh. He's the sheriff."

"I'm aware of his job title, but you also know how many citations he's given me this past year, and how many fines I've had to pay. The man has no heart."

Not exactly true, especially in light of the previous night, but the more she thought about the sheriff, the more she realized last night may have simply been an anomaly brought on by extreme circumstances. Focusing on Sheriff Wilson's past aggressions seemed to help clear him from her heart.

That had always been her problem when it came

to men. She couldn't see them for who they really were in the midst of being wooed by them…not that the sheriff was in any way wooing her…or was he?

Had last night been an elaborate scheme to win her affections so she'd let her guard down? But to what end? By all indications, he didn't like anything about her, especially her determination not to turn away stray barn animals when she knew they were outlawed within city limits.

"Maybe not for goats and pigs, but he sure does have a big heart when it comes to babies."

"That's beside the point. I deal in livestock and house pets, not babies, and if he's going to be my friend, he has to give me a break every now and then."

"So you're mad at him because last night he gave you a fine for your current menagerie?"

Coco wanted to tell her that she'd gotten a huge fine that would set her back a few months, but she hadn't gotten one. "Not exactly."

"I don't know what that means. Either he gave you a citation or he didn't."

Drew had a way of seeing things with extreme clarity, a trait Coco admired…most of the time.

"He did not give me a citation, but that doesn't mean he wasn't thinking about it. We were snowbound. What could I do about any of the animals then?"

Her face lit up, as if she'd stumbled onto the meaning of life. "So he bent the rules?"

"Kind of."

"More than just kind of. He could've still slapped you with a large fine, but he didn't. This says a lot."

Drew was jumping to conclusions that weren't grounded in anything other than wishful thinking. Truth be told, Coco knew that Drew wasn't a fan of Russ Knightly, either as a person or as a prospective mayor. Coco continually tried to change her mind, but so far all attempts had fallen on deaf ears.

"No, it doesn't."

"Yes, it does. It says that he's warming up to you. That he likes you. That he's willing to ignore his ethics for you. This is huge! I think you should cancel your date with Russ, and instead, when Sheriff Wilson shows up, you should invite him in for dinner before he takes baby Lily to wherever he has to take her. Besides, I know you're in no hurry to let this little sweetheart go."

With much care, Drew sat down on the sofa and moved Lily to her lap, laying her in the center of her legs so her tiny head was cradled between Drew's knees and her tiny feet rested against Drew's stomach. A position Lily seemed to love, and a position Coco had adopted for most of the day, both while everyone was there and once they'd left.

Punky jumped up and sat on the arm of the sofa…a perfect vantage point from which to guard the apartment.

The apartment, although rather large, could barely contain all the baby supplies that had been given to Coco for Lily. She only hoped everything would fit into Jet's SUV and they could donate it to Child Welfare when the time came.

That was if Sheriff Wilson was still planning on

going through with his plan. She hadn't heard from him all day, and hadn't wanted to call him for fear he might come and take Lily sooner rather than later. But now it was getting late, and if the sheriff didn't show up in the next fifteen minutes, Coco was contemplating leaving Drew here to deal with him and with Lily.

"Don't be ridiculous. Certainly, I'm ready to let Lily go," Coco said, but in the same breath, she realized how sad she would be once Lily was out of her life.

She suddenly felt as if Lily understood her, especially when she let out a little series of complaints. Coco went over and sat down next to Drew, and she stroked Lily's perfect silky head. "Okay, yes, it's hard to let her go…extremely hard, but there's nothing I can do about it. She's not mine to keep, but I'm sure she'll be in good hands. Someone will take her into their heart very soon. I'm sure there are hundreds of wonderful people waiting to adopt a lovely baby like Lily. And no way do I want to make dinner for the sheriff. That would bring on way too many complications."

Although now that she thought of it, she would love to spend another night with Jet and Lily. She couldn't remember the last time she'd felt so at ease with a situation as she had last night, but she would never admit that to Drew or the entire town would have them engaged by morning.

"What kind of complications? That you actually like him? Which I can tell that you do. Every time you mention his name your face lights up."

Coco abruptly stood. "That's just my new dewy makeup. It's supposed to make my face glow."

"Whatever you say." Drew checked her phone for the umpteenth time. "Isn't the sheriff cutting it close? Shouldn't he be here by now?"

Drew was right. The sheriff was way overdue. Coco banked on her contingency plan.

"I was hoping you could stay with Lily until he gets here."

"I would love to, but I'm supposed to meet up with some friends in a half hour. We're going ice-skating at Skaits. The pond is open despite all the snow, and afterward, I'm meeting Nash for hot cocoa at Holy Rollers. Matter of fact—" she picked up Lily and handed her to Coco "—I have to leave now if I'm going to have enough time to walk over there."

"You're meeting the deputy sheriff? This is the third time in the last couple of weeks."

"I know a good guy when I see him, unlike someone else I'm best friends with."

But before Coco could put up any resistance, Drew had grabbed her coat and dashed down the stairs in less time than it took for Coco to adjust Lily in her arms. Punky barked in defiance, and suddenly, Coco was once again alone with baby Lily, the child who was stealing her heart.

SHERIFF JET WILSON'S phone buzzed once again as he sat in his SUV parked across the street from Coco's place. He'd been sitting there for the past hour, in the cold, trying to wrap his head around what had to be the single most confusing news he'd ever gotten in his entire life. He'd wanted to go in and discuss it with Coco, who had called him at least four times in the past half hour, but he'd seen Drew up in her apartment through the windows and he didn't want to discuss anything either on the phone or in person while she was around. Not that he couldn't have simply asked her to leave, but that act alone would have spun some gossip, and frankly, he didn't need any more tongues wagging.

He watched as Drew exited out onto the front porch and then walked up the sidewalk to her house.

The coast was now clear.

Still, he hesitated.

He kept reading the letter over and over, not wanting to believe it, not wanting to accept it, not knowing how to accept it.

> …Lily is your daughter. I thought I could keep her and move on, but I've met someone and I can't look after a baby anymore…

When he'd first read those two sentences, he thought maybe he'd gotten the wrong letter, that perhaps it was meant for someone else…surely not for him.

Then when he read the name on the envelope again, and again, he knew Dani had written it for him. But it simply couldn't be true.

The thing was, he knew for a fact they'd never had unprotected sex, so unless Dani had purposely sabotaged one of the condoms, which he wouldn't put completely past her, or one of them was defective, which occasionally happened, Lily could not be his.

Or so he wanted desperately to believe.

He couldn't be a father. Not with his job, the state of his finances, his wacky sleep schedule. Heck, he didn't even have a place to live. And what of the townsfolk? They'd eat this stuff up and probably portray him as the bad guy. The dad was always the bad guy in these kinds of things.

At first he was angry over the letter. Why hadn't Dani confronted him in person? What kind of a mother left their baby on a cold, windy porch when the father, or who she thought was the father, lived right there in town?

But sometime during the past fifteen minutes, his attitude changed. He decided that Dani was lying, that the odds of him being the father were next to impossible. Besides, there was some doubt that she was loyal to him during the time they'd dated. He would proceed with his plans of dropping Lily off with Marsha Oberlin. He'd already called to tell her he would be late, and she was fine with it.

He felt certain that a loving family would adopt Lily. That there were probably three or four families right now waiting for her—all he had to do was drop her off with Ms. Oberlin.

Still, his mind raced with various scenarios, where Lily didn't get adopted and, just like him, she had to grow up in foster care.

And what if Dani was telling the truth? What if he was Lily's dad? How could he allow his own daughter to go into foster care? He exited his SUV just as a shiny black luxury vehicle pulled up in front of Coco's clinic. Jet knew it belonged to Russ from the custom license plate: NITE-HWK. When another man got out and walked over and rang Coco's bell, Jet knew Russ must have sent his driver to pick her up.

Undaunted, Jet made his way to the clinic just as Coco's apartment door opened. He quickly ascended the three steps to the front porch.

"Cutting it close," Coco told him as he stood behind Russ's driver, a short man with glasses, dressed in a black suit, trying to look official. "I called you several times, but you never picked up."

"You can wait in the car," Jet told the driver, who now turned, revealing a small gold name tag pinned to his jacket pocket. Jet caught the name. "Peter… Doctor Grant will be down in a few minutes."

But Peter didn't move until Coco assured him that it would be okay. "Give me about ten minutes to pass baby Lily over to the sheriff."

Peter nodded and went back to his SUV, turning over the engine, undoubtedly wanting to keep warm.

"Is Lily ready?" Jet asked as he forged his way through the open doorway. Coco, he noted right away, was wearing a lethal dress under her open coat.

He wanted this thing over with as soon as possible so everyone could get back to their separate lives.

"Yes, she just fell asleep. I put her in the car seat Amanda donated. It's for an infant, so she fits perfectly."

"Great," Jet told her, realizing he'd forgotten all

about picking up a car seat. The letter had so thrown him that it was all he could do to concentrate on driving over to Coco's clinic, much less think about getting more baby supplies along the way.

As they got farther into the apartment, aside from Punky greeting him with a frantic tail wag and jumping in front of him until he gave the tiny dog a nod of recognition and a couple hardy scratches under his ears, he couldn't help but acknowledge the place looked like a warehouse for baby stuff.

"What happened here?" he asked looking around at the clothes, toys and other gear for infants.

"Drew told a few people, and they told more folks, and before I knew it, half the town stopped by to donate to Lily."

"Don't they know that she's not staying?"

"I tried to tell them, but they insisted on Lily having it. If not, they're hoping the stuff can be donated to a children's charity."

"Fair enough, but there's no time now to search for a good outfit to donate to. I can do it tomorrow probably. For now, I just want Lily, a couple bottles of formula, a change of clothes and some diapers. I won't be able to take any more than that, and I don't even know if they'll let me give them that much."

He walked over and looked down at Lily, who was fast asleep strapped into the car seat. She seemed so helpless it about ripped out his heart just staring at her, but he told himself it was for the best. He was only doing what he had to do. There was no way he could keep her even if she was his.

"But you know she won't take any other bottle. You have to tell them about the bottle. I'd hate to have her fuss all night and not eat."

Coco put a bag together with only the things he asked for. While he waited, he tried not to look at Lily. If he didn't look at her, he might be able to steel his emotions so that he could go through with this.

Besides, what if Lily was his? What would it change? Nothing.

This was for the best.

He kept telling himself that over and over, but he didn't believe it for a moment.

"I will. I promise."

"And she doesn't like to sit when you burp her, she likes it best when she's on your shoulder. Can you tell them that, as well?"

"I think they know how to handle a baby," he said, but he had no idea who would take care of Lily. He only knew what it had been like when he'd lived with foster parents. Most of them pretended to care for a little while, at least while the representative came to check on things, but for the most part he and any other child was on his or her own.

"From what you told me, I'm not so sure."

"Then come with us and tell them for yourself, or are you too busy with Russ to think about Lily's needs, and all you want to do is pile everything on me?"

Jet knew what he'd just said was mean, but he hadn't been able to stop himself.

"That's not fair. I'm only reminding you of *her*

needs. You can do anything you want with the information."

This was going no place fast. "Is everything together? Because your driver is waiting and I'm already late. The sooner I get this over with the better for all of us."

"Except maybe for Lily," Coco spit out. Her irritation matched his.

He grabbed the handle on the car seat and swung Lily over to his side. When he went for the bag, Coco held on to it. "I'll carry this down the stairs. They're a little steep and I certainly don't want you falling while you're carrying Lily," she said.

"I won't fall." He reached for the bag, but she held it away from him, only adding to his impatience with the entire situation. "She's only an unfortunate outcome of someone's irresponsible behavior."

"You don't know that. How can you possibly know what went on with her mom? For all you know, maybe someone forced her to give up her baby, or maybe she's destitute, or maybe, just maybe, she had no other recourse."

"Or maybe Lily just didn't fit into her plans with her new boyfriend."

They stared at each other, their ire palpable between them.

"What is all of this?" Coco demanded. "Why all the anger? Did you learn something about Lily today that you're not sharing? Do you know who the mother is?"

A million reasons why he should walk out Coco's door with Lily, deliver her to the authorities and not think twice about her or Coco ever again flooded his thoughts. But through it all, he remembered that Coco was the first woman he'd ever been completely honest with in his entire adult life. She'd been kind, compassionate and understanding, just as he'd been to her. They'd shared a moment, a time of complete honesty.

Was he willing to throw it all away on principle?

"Yes, but...I have to go."

He turned to leave.

"You can't do this. You can't leave and not tell me the truth about Lily. I deserve that much. It's only fair after everything we shared with her in the last twenty-four hours."

"That doesn't give you any rights, Doctor Grant." He couldn't bring himself to tell her the truth. If he did then it would be real, and he didn't know if he was ready for reality.

"So now I'm Doctor Grant again?" She folded her arms across her chest. "Is that how you want to end this? Maybe you should give me a citation for harboring a baby. After all, I'm not legally equipped to keep a child. I'm more the llama type."

That brought about a smile. "You don't give up, do you?"

"I can be quite scrappy. And you'll have to contend with Punky, as well."

He hadn't noticed it before, but Punky stood in front of the door, his teeth bared, looking as if he wanted to take a chunk out of the sheriff...a tiny chunk, but a chunk nonetheless.

"I can have you arrested for this, you know. Your dog is hindering my departure."

"He's only protecting Lily's best interests."

As crazy as this was, Jet refused to back down.

He went for the doorknob and Punky bit into his trousers, pulling on them with all his might. His small feet slid on the wooden floor—he'd lose traction and have to start all over again. Jet looked down at the dog, then up at Coco. "You're kidding, right?"

"Punky is a force to be reckoned with."

"Fine," Jet said, finally giving in to the absurdity of the situation. "I'll tell you, but call off your attack dog before he pulls out a tooth."

She gave Punky a command to sit and stay, and he followed her orders to the letter. Then Jet gently placed a still-sleeping Lily on the table, went over to the sofa and sat down.

"Do you have any more of that scotch?"

"I do," she told him.

"Then I think you should pour us both a glass."

"I have a feeling this is going to take a while. Maybe I should call Russ and tell him I'm going to be late."

"That's up to you."

"Before I do that, can you give me a hint as to what this is all about?"

"Lily might be my daughter," Jet said as Coco poured the scotch into two glasses. She drank hers down in one go and then picked up her phone.

"Russ, hi," she said in a strong, no-nonsense voice.

"Something important has come up, and I'm sorry, but I'm going to have to cancel our date tonight."

Then she disconnected, poured herself another scotch, walked over to the sofa and sat down next to Jet, tucking her feet under her bottom.

"So start at the beginning. I've got all night."

Chapter Six

"I keep causing you to break your dates with Russ," Jet told Coco as he sat next to her on the sofa, his legs stretched out in front of him. Boots, coat and hat all had been placed near the front door.

"No worries," Coco told him, now much more comfortable in checkered red-and-gray tights and a bright red oversize sweatshirt. They shared a plate of assorted cheese, sliced pears, apples and chunks of French bread that Coco had put together for a light dinner. "Russ understands. Heaven knows he's broken his share of dates with me."

She thought about last Saturday night when she'd raced home from a ranch almost thirty miles outside town so she could meet him at Belly Up, only to be told he'd forgotten about a fund-raiser in Jackson Hole that he needed to attend. When she questioned him on it, he'd blamed the mix-up on his assistant, who he always seemed to use as an excuse. Sometimes it made her wonder if there was something else going on.

"Not to be nosey, but how close are you and Russ?

I mean, this is the second night you've canceled because of me. If we were dating, I'd be concerned."

She didn't know how honest she wanted to be about Russ, but she also knew Jet wouldn't go spreading the truth around town. Coco liked the fact that everyone seemed to be thinking they were more serious than they actually were.

"We're just getting to know each other, in the early stages of dating. No real commitments, yet."

She wanted him to know that the potential was still there, even if they hadn't taken that next step, which was none of his business, anyway.

"Ah, now it makes sense."

"What makes sense?"

She took a little offense. Did he know more than he was letting on?

Jet fidgeted, as if something was bothering him. "Nothing. I just thought you two were in a serious relationship. You know how this town likes to talk."

"I do, and this whole thing with you and Lily could rip through our town like wildfire on dry grass. So, tell me, since we're talking relationships, are you still in love with or have feelings for Lily's mother? I mean, maybe the two of you should try to work this out. For Lily's sake."

An important fact, considering her earlier thoughts about the sheriff…not that she was actually pondering having any kind of committed relationship with Sheriff Wilson. Still, she wanted to know where he stood, emotionally.

He shook his head. "Not possible. That ended a long time ago."

"You don't have to tell me who she is, but is it someone I'm going to bump into around town?"

The thought of running into the woman who gave up Lily made her pause.

"It's Dani Century, and as you probably know, she moved away months ago. I have no intention of working anything out with her. Besides, according to her note, she's with somebody else. Thing is, I don't see how any of this is possible. We always used protection."

Dani Century had breezed back into Briggs for about three months, then left one afternoon in a hurry. If memory served Coco right, she'd taken off with a cowboy who was busy learning the rodeo circuit and wanted Coco's brother, Carson, to teach him how to ride a bronc. Carson knew right off he wasn't serious and told him so up front. They both departed shortly after that.

"You know there's always a slight chance..." She didn't feel comfortable finishing the thought. "Well, sometimes there's a fault in the... I'm only saying."

With all her veterinary training, and all the foals and calves and kids she'd delivered, talking about sex still made her uncomfortable.

"Yeah, but come on...that's so rare."

"Apparently not rare enough," she chided. "But if you feel as though she's lying, you and Lily can always take a DNA test, just to be certain. The results can be had in a few days. That way you'll know for certain."

"That's true, but what do I do while I'm waiting? And, if I could help it, I really don't want anyone to know about this." He raked his hand through his hair and she noticed how his upper arm bulged under his shirt. The thought of his ripped chest sent her mind racing with sinful thoughts and she had to force herself to reel her mind back to the present problem.

"Well, if there's even a remote chance she's yours, you can't turn her over to Child Protective Services. There's no telling what would happen if you did. I'm sorry, but it seems like you're going to have to keep her until you can get the results of the test."

Coco felt as though she was making perfect sense, even for the stubborn, by-the-book sheriff.

"That's the problem. Actually, it's a twofold problem. I don't have anywhere to live. I've been sleeping at the jail while my landlord fixes a broken water pipe, which was supposed to have been taken care of early this week. With all this snow, who knows when it'll get fixed? The pipe is under the house.

"Plus, with my schedule, how the heck am I supposed to take care of an infant? She requires constant care and most of my day is spent out of the office. This will never work."

Coco thought for a moment, desperately wanting to help Jet and baby Lily, who she'd fallen completely in love with.

"My parents always taught me that all problems

have solutions, you just have to dig deep enough to find them."

He drank down his scotch, then looked over at her. His deep brown eyes appeared almost completely black in the low lighting of her apartment.

"I can appreciate the sentiment, but my upbringing serves as the perfect example of how that theory doesn't work."

"On the contrary, it's the perfect example of how it *did* work. Maybe not for your ideal way of thinking, but you weren't homeless or starving. The solution was to put you in foster care."

"So, after all that I've told you, you believe I should still turn Lily over? Is that what you're saying? I thought you were opposed to that."

"I am. We're not digging deep enough, but I may have a temporary solution, at least until your apartment is livable again and you can learn the truth about Lily. You and Lily can stay here!"

He smirked and looked down at the floor for a moment, obviously contemplating what she'd just suggested.

"As much as I appreciate the generous offer, this sofa is by far one of the most uncomfortable pieces of furniture I've ever sat on, much less tried to sleep on. And, even though we haven't discussed it, I can't keep sleeping with you. Besides, I don't think Russ would like it."

The thought of waking up every morning lying next to Jet Wilson was more than she wanted to contemplate.

She immediately told him her idea. "Obviously neither of those will work. However, I have a spare bedroom that I use for some storage and for my office, but you could buy one of those super air mattresses—they're exactly the size of a queen-size bed—and I can move my laptop anywhere. Lily can continue to sleep with me. I love having her share my room, so that's not a problem."

"Do you understand all the ramifications of that arrangement? It's one thing for me to have a scandal, but if Lily and I move in for a few days, that scandal will grow to epic proportions. Are you ready to take that on?"

She knew it was risky, but it seemed like the best idea for everyone involved. Russ was a tolerant man. She felt certain he'd understand. Besides, it gave her more time with Lily, and that alone made her happy.

"Let them talk. It gives them something to do other than focus on the weather."

"It could hurt your relationship with Russ."

"I can take care of Russ. He's an open-minded man. He'll understand."

Jet looked skeptical. "There are a lot of words I would use to describe Russ Knightly, but *open-minded* isn't on the list."

"You don't know him like I do," she said, defending Russ. She truly believed that tolerance was one of his best qualities. Jet simply had the wrong opinion of him.

"If you say so, but let's not forget that Lily wakes

up a lot during the night. I don't care about my sleep, but it's not fair to you."

"I don't mind. I'm used to it with all the emergency calls I get. Some of the animals are sick and require medication in the middle of the night. Besides, you and I can take turns feeding Lily."

His face began to soften, and she could see that his entire body was beginning to relax.

"Okay, I can see how this might work, for a while, but we both have outdoor day jobs. What do we do with Lily while we're running around the valley?"

"I can take her with me when I know my day won't be too intense. She's not a burden. And if I can't, I know Drew would love to babysit her. And maybe Nash can take on more of the outdoor problems, and you can take Lily with you to the jail for a few hours."

Shaking his head, he pushed himself up on the sofa. "I don't like children in a police station, much less near a jail cell. You never know what might happen."

"Well, then, maybe you can work from here for a few hours a day. Transfer any phone calls to your personal phone instead of an answering service."

He folded his arms on his chest, showing his last bits of resistance to the idea.

"I don't know," he said with a slight crack in his voice. "It's a lot to put on you. Why would you do this?"

"Because Lily deserves the best possible chance at life."

"And you think I can give it to her?"

"I do," she told him, looking straight into his eyes. "You'll be a great father to Lily."

He looked away. "I'm the last person she needs as her father. Lily deserves two parents who love her, who can raise her together. She should have a father who doesn't have a dangerous job, and a mom who won't run out on her for another guy."

"She does, but for now, you're all she has, and after that DNA test comes in, she may not even have you. But for the next few days I'm willing to give her all the love I have…if you are."

"Either way, this is a tough decision."

Lily started to fuss, with little groans and complaints.

"It's either my solution or you should be packing Lily up soon, because it's a long drive with a screaming baby."

Lily began to wail, and they both jumped up to take care of her at the same time. Coco unfastened her from the seat and picked her up to love her.

"I'll make the bottle," Jet said, a wide grin warming his face.

"I'll take care of her diaper," Coco told him, satisfied she'd changed his mind.

It was then that Coco realized that for the next several days, she, Lily and Sheriff Wilson would be playing family. She only hoped she hadn't just set herself up for a huge heartbreak…with Russ.

BRIGHT AND EARLY the next morning, after Jet had showered, dressed, changed and fed Lily, then left for the day, Coco cleared out the boxes in the spare bedroom. Lily slept as Coco stored what items she could in her walk-in closet, and the rest of the containers downstairs in the clinic. Though, as soon as the animals heard her rattling around, they all started clamoring for food and attention, which she gladly gave them. She let the kittens, the piglet and the puppy out of their respective cages for some much-needed playtime. They'd have to be adopted out soon, she realized. She didn't have the heart to keep them penned up all day.

Funny thing about baby animals, they all got along usually once they'd given each other a good sniff. Even the llamas enjoyed playing with the puppy that at once tried to show his dominance, only to be shot down by a couple strong nudges.

Coco checked her messages and learned that her sister Kenzie, who managed the Grant family ranch, would be able to stop by this week to pick up the farm animals.

Then she checked on her appointments. She had three, but was able to push them off until tomorrow, when she knew all the back roads would be cleared enough to navigate safely. Fortunately, she only had a couple of appointments in her clinic that afternoon, so keeping Lily with her wasn't going to be a problem.

She thought she'd spend part of the morning getting everything ready for Jet and then manage a late breakfast with Russ at Holy Rollers, the local bakery. Next to her mom's cookies and cakes, the items in this place were her absolute favorite.

Russ and Coco took a private table inside the bakery, which prided itself on offering almost any kind of baked good a patron could want.

"How long did you say Lily and the sheriff would be staying at your apartment?" Russ asked for the second time.

Coco sipped on a mocha latte while Russ drank a cup of iced black coffee. They shared a plain oatmeal muffin, not exactly Coco's first choice, but Russ had ordered it before she'd had a say in the matter. She'd gone back and ordered a dozen assorted doughnuts to go, and had already stuffed the box in her SUV for later. She now knew Jet liked doughnuts, especially the custard-filled kind that she enjoyed, with thick chocolate frosting. They both liked chocolate frosting. The owner of Holy Rollers, Amanda Gump, who had generously donated the car seat to Lily, who always had a good word for everyone she knew, had offered up all this doughnut information without Coco having to tell her why she wanted to know.

The cozy shop buzzed with the usual morning rush, as customers hovered over the glass display counters waiting for their morning shot of sugar and caffeine. Holy Rollers was *the* morning hangout for all ages. Coco couldn't get through a week without stopping in at least three times for a latte and her usual cream-filled, chocolate-covered doughnut, a treat she was anxious to get to once she got back home.

"Only for about three or four days," Coco told him, trying her best to convince him that this was a good idea and truly believing that once Russ knew all the facts, he'd be on her side. After all, Russ was a reasonable man, a man of virtue. Why else would he be running for mayor and doing so well in the polls? The good people of Briggs would never elect someone who didn't exemplify their moral code. "Just until his apartment is livable again. Right now, there's no water due to a broken pipe."

Baby Lily slept in her donated car seat on a chair next to Coco. Outside, the sun tried its best to melt the snow, but the cold temperature wouldn't cooperate.

"So, let me get this straight. Tilly might be the sheriff's baby?"

"It's Lily, and yes. Dani Century is the mom, but we really shouldn't be talking about this here." She looked around to see if anyone was close enough to listen in on their conversation. "Sheriff Wilson doesn't want this news to get out."

"Huh. And he claims he had no idea about any of this?"

"He's not even certain that Lily is his. He's getting a DNA test to prove it one way or the other."

Russ snickered and shook his head as he drank his coffee. "Gotta hand it to the sheriff. Never thought he'd be a part of something like this. A reckless scandal of the year for ol' Briggs, Idaho."

"It's not a scandal, at least not yet. No one knows about it but you and me, and I only told you because I know I can trust you. And I wanted to make sure you understood all the facts of why Jet's staying with me. But it has no bearing on our relationship. Matter of fact, I hope our date is still on for tonight."

"Of course it is. My only concern is how this might look to the good people of Briggs…the sheriff moving in with my girl. Might cause a lot of speculation, a lot of unnecessary gossip."

"Not if we don't tell anyone. It we play it right, by the time the gossip leaks, Sheriff Wilson and Lily will have already moved out."

"Yes, but I…"

Russ kept getting distracted by friends and acquaintances who wanted to wish him a good morning or talk to him about anything from extending the Western Days festival to adding a streetlight on Main and First.

"Excuse me, Mr. Knightly, but we sure could'a used those extra plows in the last couple'a days," Marty Bean, owner of Moo's Creamery, said in a loud voice. "You've got my vote, that's for sure."

"Thanks," Russ told him, turning to shake his hand. "I appreciate it. There's so many more community improvements I want to make. You're going to be amazed at how efficient this town runs after I'm elected."

"Looking forward to it," Kerry Walker, the local cobbler, told him, holding on to a paper cup filled with a hot beverage and carrying a pink box of pastries.

It had been like that ever since she and Russ sat down. People kept coming up to their table to wish him well with the election that was less than two weeks away. Great for Russ, but not so great for a serious conversation with him.

"Is this Lily?" Betty Hastings, an older woman, asked. "I heard all about her from Amanda Gump. Poor little dear. Glad you're both taking such good care of her."

"It's our pleasure, especially while the sheriff is so busy," Russ told her.

Coco's stomach did a flip and her throat tightened. She gave Russ a look, but he seemed to ignore her.

"Our sheriff has enough on his plate without having to look for Lily's mom," Kerry Walker said. "Poor darlin' needs her mom."

"She sure does," Russ announced, as he gazed lovingly over at Lily. It was the first time he'd really looked at her since she and Coco had arrived almost an hour ago. "And her dad."

Panic tightened Coco's chest and she could feel her eyes go wide. Hadn't she been clear enough that Jet's paternity was a secret?

"Whoever that is," seventysomething Phyllis Gabaur added. Phyllis was by far the town's biggest and best gossip. If anyone wanted to spread a rumor, they could just say something in front of Phyllis and it would travel faster than if it had been written in the sky.

"Didn't you know?" Russ began, looking over at Coco, who shook her head. "Oh, wait, that information might be a secret. Is it private and confidential, darling?"

Coco hated this.

"Actually…"

"I love secrets," Phyllis said.

I bet you do, Coco thought. "We're all simply waiting to learn information about Lily like everyone else. There's no secret," Coco said, trying her best to quell the storm and not pique anyone's interest. If Phyllis thought there was a secret, she would be relentless until she learned its origin.

Russ turned, set his focus squarely on Coco and with a reassuring voice said, "Oh, well, in that case, if it's not a secret that Sheriff Wilson is the father—"

"*Might* be the father," Coco said, leaping to the sheriff's defense. "Wait…no… We can't be…" She clammed up, but she couldn't take back the words.

"*Our* sheriff is the father? Well, I'll be," Phyllis said, and slipped away like dust in the wind. One minute she was there, ogling baby Lily, and once she had her tidbit of gossip, she vanished.

Coco's heart raced, and as if on cue, Lily stretched her arms and legs, and opened her eyes.

"Wow, Sheriff Wilson has a baby," Betty said. "That's wonderful news!"

And with that, questions came rapid-fire, but Lily wanted no part of it. Her wails permeated the shop, and soon everyone in it, including the staff, stared at Lily. Coco wanted to get out of there. Fast. The damage was more than done.

She slipped on her coat and collected Lily, and without Russ even noticing, she stepped out of Holy Rollers. She needed to find somewhere to feed Lily, and then she wanted to meet up with Jet and explain

what had just happened before he heard it from almost anyone.

Coco picked up her pace.

"WHY DIDN'T YOU tell me you were the father?" Cindy
Whipple asked as she rung up Jet's only item—
earplugs. Several customers walked up and down the
aisles collecting items in their baskets, but Jet knew
they were doing their best to listen to the conversation he was having with Mrs. Whipple.

"Excuse me?" He wasn't sure he'd heard her correctly. The register was making too much noise. He
knew she'd said something about a father, but he
wasn't sure in what context.

"Baby Lily… The other night when you stopped
by for all those baby things…why didn't you tell me
you were her father?"

He did a mental shudder, almost in disbelief that
she already knew about the letter, and he wondered
how that was even possible. It was barely noon. How
in the devil could it have gotten out and spread so
quickly? He'd only told Coco and from the way she'd
talked last night, there was no chance she would have
passed that information around. She knew how he felt
about it. How unsure he was that Lily was actually
his. She wouldn't do that to him.

Would she?

"There's more to the story," he told Cindy while
handing her a five-dollar bill.

She made change. "Like what? I'd love to hear it.
And I was right about the mom being one of them

Century girls, wasn't I? I'm pretty good when it comes to these kinds of things. Got a sixth sense. Should have been one of them fortune-tellers. Might have made a lot more money reading tarot cards than opening a corner market. Although I still can't figure out why a man like you ever got mixed up with the likes of one of those girls. Makes me wonder who you really are under that badge you wear on your chest every day."

"I'm just a man, Mrs. Whipple, like every other man in this valley."

She handed him his change and nodded, a knowing look in her eyes. "You mean you're a horny toad?"

By now everyone in the store was standing around, listening to them talk.

He took his change and grabbed the earplugs off the counter. "Good day to you then, Mrs. Whipple."

"Well, now that you're living with Doctor Grant, don't you go gettin' her in a family way, as well. She's a proper veterinary doctor, she'll be wise to your seducin' ways. Besides, she's dating Russ Knightly and if things keep going the way they are, she could be our first lady. Everybody knows that."

"I'll keep that in mind and try to keep myself in check," he said and stalked out of the store, with everyone snickering as they stared at him.

"Is that a promise?" Cindy Whipple hollered after him.

Never turning around, he hotfooted it out of the store.

Once he stepped outside, he suddenly noticed how some of the townsfolk were staring at him, smirking with each hello. He hadn't thought anything of it earlier when he'd gone into Holy Rollers for coffee and a cream-filled doughnut. He figured everyone was merely being nice after all he and his deputy had done during the past couple of days, what with the big snowstorm.

But now he knew the truth. They were gossiping about his connection to Lily.

Coco had probably spilled his secret to someone, maybe Drew, and it had spread exactly like he had predicted. He wanted to lash out at Coco for spilling the information. He thought for sure she would hold it close at least for a couple days.

Apparently, she hadn't.

He couldn't figure her out. When they were together, he thought for sure there were some embers burning, if nothing else, at least the embers of a solid friendship. Then, as soon as she was out on her own, she'd turned on him. Betrayed his trust. But maybe there never was any trust. Maybe he'd been played for some crazy reason he couldn't quite understand. Maybe it had something to do with the election. With Russ. With her inner desire for power.

He knew he was probably thinking off the deep end.

It didn't make any sense, especially since he'd loaded up his SUV with enough of his things for several days, and he'd found an air bed at Hess's Department Store like she'd told him about, bought it, and he was just about to bring it over to Coco's apartment and set it up in that spare bedroom she'd talked about.

But now he wasn't sure that he should.

Why would she invite him in, appear as if she had his back, if she was simply going to stick a knife in it?

He couldn't begin to imagine her motives.

For a man who valued his privacy...treasured his privacy...all the details of his now scandalous affair had instantly become fodder for the town's busybodies.

As he hurried back to his vehicle down the now cleaned sidewalks, past the open-for-business shops on Main Street, trying to get a handle on all of this, total confusion muddied up his thoughts.

He'd known this would happen eventually, just not the first day.

He beeped open the SUV and jumped inside, shutting out the town around him, trying his best to understand what this all meant.

Chapter Seven

For the next couple of days, Jet and Coco were polite and mindful of each other's privacy, circumstances that Jet appreciated. Circumstances that he knew were only temporary. He went about his business, and she went about hers, meeting only at night for dinner, a situation he didn't fully understand, given how, until recently, Russ had buzzed around her like a bee to a flower.

Not that he was complaining about the situation. He wasn't. Matter of fact, he truly enjoyed their dinners, and was looking forward to one tonight, but he found it curious nonetheless and continued to keep his distance.

They hadn't discussed how the town had learned about his letter from Dani, because it never came up in conversation. Every time something even remotely close to that subject was mentioned, one of them would quickly change the subject. And for the time being, Jet could live with that just fine.

Plus, he didn't press his luck. He tried to be gone when Coco woke up in the morning, dropping Lily off with Drew and her folks whenever possible. Sometimes, like yesterday, Coco had packed up and left with Lily before he'd stepped out of his room, which was okay with him. He had also learned how to pack up Lily with everything she needed and take her with him when all he had to do was attend a council meeting or participate in a school function.

He even managed to set up a DNA test with Lily without anyone, even Coco, knowing what he was up to. He wanted to keep the test a secret for as long as possible. Not that everyone didn't already think he was the father—he just didn't want them betting on the results, which he knew for a fact they would do.

He'd made the appointment with Doctor Bradley Starr, the town's general practitioner, for a Saturday afternoon, when he knew Coco would be out tending to two new stallions on one of the outlying ranches and couldn't take Lily along. There were virtually no internet or phone signals out there, and Coco didn't want to put Lily in that kind of situation, especially while out in the pastures.

The doctor agreed to have them come into the office when no one, not even his nurse, would be around. They could meet in complete privacy.

"From all indications, Lily is about three weeks old, maybe closer to four," Doctor Starr said. "Her weight is right on target, and in general, she's in very good health. We should get the results of the DNA test in about five to ten business days."

Jet did up Lily's pink jumper, then slipped on her warm funny monkey outer jumper and zipped it up.

When she was all nice and toasty, hood fastened, hands completely covered, Jet secured her in her car seat.

"There you go, sweet cakes. You're all set." He looked over at the doctor. "That's great news on all fronts, Doc. Thanks."

Lily had barely fussed during the exam, and now she was busy looking around at all the bright pictures and mobiles that dominated the small examination room. Even though Doctor Starr was a GP, he treated most of the babies and children in the town, so he kept one of his examination rooms dedicated to those patients.

"I'll send the results over to the station when they come in. Will that be okay?"

"Yes. Thanks. And if it's possible, I would so like it if you could keep all of this to yourself."

"Sure thing, but how are you coping with the possibility, Jet? Everything okay?"

Jet and Doctor Starr had been building a friendship of sorts ever since Jet had first come to town. Not only was the doctor his personal physician, but on the first Friday of every month some of the guys in town would play poker at Belly Up. Although no money would ever change hands in any of the games the sheriff participated in, at least.

"Doing fine, just fine. No worries there."

"Have you thought about what you're going to do if Lily is yours? And what kind of relationship you'll have with her mother?"

"I'll cross that bridge when I come to it, but for

now, Dani has moved on. We won't be having a relationship."

Jet shrugged on his coat and secured his hat on his head. He was in no mood to discuss the scenario with the doctor or anyone, for that matter.

"Then have you thought about how you'll take care of Lily? Raising a child is a big responsibility, Jet."

"Believe me, I'm fully aware of that."

"It would mean moving to a bigger place. That thimble of an apartment you live in now won't cut it. And you'll need to hire a full-time nanny. Admittedly the city doesn't pay you very much, so that expense alone will be tough, not to mention all the other costs of raising a child."

He picked up Lily's car seat. "Doc, I appreciate everything you're saying. Really, I do. But in my line of work, I can't afford the luxury of 'what if.' I only deal in the facts, and right now, there are no facts supporting Dani's claim. And until paternity is proven, one way or the other, all I can do is provide Lily with a safe and loving environment."

The doctor rested his hand on Jet's shoulder. "All well and good, Sheriff Wilson, but I can see that Lily has already stolen your heart. I'm thinking if it's proven that she's not your child that will be harder on you than if she is."

Jet hated the fact that Doctor Starr might be right. No matter how hard he tried to steel his feelings for Lily, whenever she did something new, or reacted to his voice, she stole a piece of him that would always be hers.

"Either way, I'm fine."

Jet shook hands with the doctor and snuck out of the office through the back door, knowing perfectly well that someone might see him coming out of the front door, which was right on Main Street.

Before he stepped one foot outside, he was about to toss a blanket over the top of the car seat to shield Lily from the cold wind, but that sweet little baby seemed to be looking right at him, making him sigh on the spot.

Not only was he falling for Lily, but despite himself, he was falling for Coco just as hard.

"THESE LITTLE GUYS are perfect," Kenzie told her sister Coco as they loaded the baby llamas onto Kenzie's horse trailer.

Coco was thrilled her sister had driven in to get them, but she had a hard time concentrating on what her sister was saying. Ever since Russ had betrayed her secret about the sheriff and Lily—if it was a betrayal—she hadn't been able to think about him in the same light. That question had her thoughts in such a tangle that she had a hard time concentrating on anything else.

"That's nice," Coco mumbled without hearing everything that Kenzie had said.

"I've been thinking about getting a couple llamas to add to our livestock," Kenzie continued. "The coyote population is getting mighty restless and encroaching on the ranch at a steady pace. These little guys will help ward them off. They just need a couple more months to grow, and they'll be a formidable deterrent."

"Good idea," Coco told her.

"Are you actually listening to me?"

The sisters stood behind Coco's clinic in the clearing they'd made through the snow. For her part, Kenzie backed up that trailer like a pro, only requiring a minimal amount of direction. Something Coco could never do. She could barely back up her SUV, let alone an entire trailer.

"Of course I am. The llamas are a formidable deterrent."

Kenzie looked all warm and cozy in a hooded, deep red down-filled parka, jeans and her usual tan-colored cowgirl boots. Even in the dead of winter, with several feet of snow on the ground, Kenzie never wore anything but a sturdy pair of boots. Her makeup was minimal, and her long, almost black hair was clipped up. Thick work gloves covered her hands, and a black scarf encircled her neck.

"Is everything okay? You seem very distracted. For one thing, it's colder than a cave out here and you're wearing a summer jacket."

Without thinking about it, Coco had slipped on the thin jacket that always hung on a hook next to the back door. No scarf, no gloves, but she did manage to step into her favorite black lace-up, calf-high boots. No cowgirl boots for her. She found them completely uncomfortable and useless for the kind of work she did.

"I'm fine. Just didn't feel like running back upstairs for my coat, is all. We're almost done here, anyway."

Unfortunately, this move was taking longer than Coco had anticipated. The cold had wrapped around her like a vise and chilled her to her very bones. Despite feeling frigid, she helped to load the animals, imagining it would only take a few more minutes, so she could stand the frosty conditions. Besides, she couldn't stop thinking about Russ's attitude the other morning at Holy Rollers. What was that all about? Had she somehow misjudged him?

She kept knocking that hour at Holy Rollers around in her mind, sure that she'd told him to keep the sheriff's information a secret.

Or maybe she hadn't made herself clear? Why else could he have gotten so confused and told everyone the details?

Her mind fogged up like a mirror in a steamy bathroom every time she thought about it. She couldn't see past the betrayal, his eagerness to tell the group all the details surrounding the sheriff and baby Lily. It was almost as though he'd delighted in having something scandalous to share about the sheriff.

How could that possibly be true? She'd wanted to talk to him about it, but whenever she'd called, he'd been too busy to discuss it. Fortunately, they had a date that night. She was hoping to clear the air so they could get on with their relationship, because as it stood now, she could hardly think of him without getting completely frustrated.

The goats' bleating brought her back to the present and she noticed that Kenzie was giving the kids a healthy snack.

"Sure you don't want to adopt those fellas, as well?" Coco asked, hoping her sister would change her mind and say yes. Finding a forever home for goats at this time of year was tough. They ate like crazy, and with no grazing land available due to the weather, most ranchers didn't want two more mouths to feed.

"At this point, despite them being adorably sweet, they're a liability. It's a shame. I'll take them for now, though, to get them out of your clinic so Sheriff Wilson doesn't give you another fine, but it's a temporary situation…for a few weeks max. You'll have to find them and the piglet a permanent home after that."

Coco's teeth chattered from the bitter cold.

"There's one more thing I should tell you before you go, and I'm surprised you haven't heard about it already. Maybe you should come inside for this. It's complicated, and I'm really freezing."

Coco wanted to get warm. Her ears felt a bit numb, and her insides couldn't stop shaking. She crossed her arms over her chest and hugged herself for warmth.

"Sorry, sis." Kenzie fished out the key for her truck from her pocket. "We've been snowed in until today, remember? We've been so busy, it's a wonder I had time to drive into town for the animals. As it is, I can't even sit for a visit. I need to turn right around and drive back. The heavy snow destroyed one of our hay sheds. Everyone's working hard to repair it.

I need to get home and help. Can you give me the short version?"

Coco took in a deep breath, wanting to get it all out in one big push. The bitter wind stung as she breathed. "Sheriff Wilson might be the father to a three-week-old baby that was left on my doorstep a few nights ago, and because he doesn't have anywhere else to stay, he's moved into my spare room. It's completely platonic, I can assure you. Oh, and somehow Russ thought I said it wasn't a secret, and now the entire town knows all the details, but I haven't told Jet how that happened yet."

"Jet? You're on a first-name basis with the sheriff?"

"After all I said, that's what you're most interested in?"

"It's the most important part of the story. Last I heard, you and Russ were an item. If I know anything about Russ Knightly and his swollen ego, he can't be good with this situation. Is it any wonder he blabbed it all over town?"

"He didn't blab it all over town, exactly. It just came out when Phyllis and a few other people happened to be standing around our table, meeting Lily."

"Who's Lily?"

"Pay attention, would you?" Coco's hands ached from the cold. She needed to go inside. "Lily is Jet's baby."

"I thought you said he didn't know if the baby is his?"

"He doesn't."

"Then why did you just tell me that Lily is Jet's baby?"

"I don't know what I'm saying. I'm too cold to think. And this is a potential crisis. I'm having a relationship meltdown. I need your input."

"This thing with Jet sounds complicated. Especially when you bring Russ into the equation. Everybody knows there's no love lost between those two men."

Coco shivered. "Russ has been nothing but a gentleman."

"I wish I could help you out more." Kenzie walked to the front of her truck with Coco following close behind, amazed that her feet still held up her freezing body. "A gentleman wouldn't spread all those private details about the sheriff." Kenzie stopped, shrugged and gave her sister a hug. "Maybe you should talk to Mom, or Carson might be better. He's always good at sorting out these kinds of things. And get indoors. You feel like a popsicle." She glanced back at the house, gesturing with her eyes. "And speaking of Sheriff Jet Wilson, isn't that him standing in your doorway?"

Coco whirled around, and sure enough, there was the sheriff looking as handsome as ever. Lately, every time she saw him, her knees went a little weak.

"What's he doing here?" Coco asked out loud. "He's not due until later tonight."

"Last I heard, he lives here, Doctor Grant. Now go on before you freeze to death. And call Mom or Carson... On second thought, why not talk it over with Jet? The way he's looking at you, there might be more to this platonic living arrangement of yours than you realize."

"What's that supposed to mean?"

But Kenzie didn't answer and instead stepped up inside the cab, slammed her door shut, turned over the ignition and drove away, leaving Coco to her own devices. Truly a situation she didn't want to be in.

KENZIE HAD DRIVEN off before Jet even had a chance to say hello. Somehow, by her quick departure, Jet had the feeling she knew about all the stories floating around town concerning Lily, and Dani. Probably not a situation she wanted to get involved in.

Smart woman.

By the time Coco slowly made her way back inside, closed the door, then didn't move, Jet knew something was wrong. She wasn't wearing a hat or gloves, and her coat looked like something you'd put on for a mild spring day, not for a winter cold snap in Idaho.

"Are you all right?" he asked, trying to get a look at her face.

She turned to him. "I…I'm…"

He took her hand in his and immediately knew what was wrong. She was colder than a calf caught in a snowdrift.

Without giving it another thought, he pulled her in tight against his body and wrapped her in his arms.

He expected some kind of resistance, but instead

she immediately tucked herself in even closer, apparently starved for warmth.

He checked her pulse… It seemed too slow.

"The Fitzpatrick family taught me all about symptoms of hypothermia and how to treat someone who might be suffering from it. Dan Fitzpatrick, the dad, was part of a mountain rescue team. From what I learned, I'd say you were in the beginning stages."

"I'm…I'm…so cold," she said in a whisper, her entire body quivering. "I…should've come inside, but…I'm so tired."

He rubbed his hands up and down her back. "Don't try to talk. Just lean into me." He pulled his wool parka up around her. "This coat you're wearing wouldn't keep a kitten warm, much less a grown woman. What were you thinking?"

"That's just it… I haven't been…thinking. I'm… sorry about…"

But she couldn't finish her sentence. She was shaking so hard he thought she might break, but the shaking was a good sign. Her body's heat regulation system was still working. "It's fine, just let me take care of you."

"Okay," she said and collapsed into him. He picked her up and carried her upstairs, her head resting on his shoulder. "You can't be…"

"Hush for a minute, we need to get you warm before hypothermia sets in, remember? You can say whatever you want once your temperature comes back up to normal."

She felt as light as a feather in his arms, and being

this close only raised his awareness of how much he genuinely cared for her. Sure he was mad as a bull standing in front of a red cape now that the entire town knew his personal business, but that didn't mean he wasn't attracted to her like all get-out.

She smelled clean, like fresh snow, with a hint of flowers, maybe roses. He liked being this close to her, just as he had liked her falling asleep on his shoulder the other night. She was a woman who brought up all sorts of emotions in him, and most of them had to do with making love to her.

But he didn't have time to dwell on any of those feelings. He needed to get her temperature up because it seemed to be falling fast.

She tucked her hands inside his open coat for relief. They felt like little icicles against his chest. Her entire body was icy.

Not good.

He took the stairs two at a time. When he walked into her apartment, with Punky at his heels, he headed straight for her bed and set her down, covering her with the comforter and every other blanket he could find. The tips of her ears were pure white. He tucked her in good and tight, making sure her shoulders and neck were covered. Then he reached under the blankets, unlaced her boots and slipped them off.

Punky used his step stool to jump up on the bed and licked her face. Then he cuddled up next to her, as if he knew something was wrong.

"Thanks," Coco said. "But…you don't have to make such a…fuss. I'll be fine."

She seemed so small and helpless, when he knew she was anything but. It always struck him how vulnerable a person looked when their health was compromised. They could be the toughest person around, attitude off the charts with bulging muscles, but when they were hurting, everything changed. All their human frailties took over, and that person was as vulnerable as those baby goats Kenzie had just carted away.

"It's no problem. Are you warming up?" he asked. "Or are you still cold?"

He figured she was finally getting warm, the shivering had subsided substantially, but he wanted to know for sure.

"Much better," she told him with a half smile. He noticed that her ears were beginning to get a rosy glow once again, and he relaxed thinking he'd caught her in time. He'd seen firsthand what hypothermia could do to a person. Not a pretty sight. Dan Fitzpatrick had taken him on one of the team's training rescue missions. He'd learned a lot. A person could die or lose limbs because of hypothermia, or just be sick for quite some time. Not that she had been close to having hypothermia, but certainly another ten or fifteen minutes out there, and she would have been a prime candidate.

Once he got a fire going in the fireplace, he put the kettle on, and by the time she could sit up and have her first sip of hot tea with honey, the shaking had completely stopped. She was able now to speak and pet Punky, who seemed to love the attention.

"Thanks for all of this. No one has done so much for me since my mom took care of me when I was living at home, and that was a lot of years ago."

He tugged off his coat and tossed it over a wicker rocking chair in the corner of the room, along with his hat. He had already locked his weapon away. Then he sat on the bed next to her, gave Punky some loving and leaned back on the headboard.

"You're welcome, but you shouldn't have let yourself get so cold. Being a doctor, you know better than that."

She nodded, holding her cup with both hands. "My fingers are actually tingling."

The blanket slipped from her shoulder and he reached over and gently covered her again. It was then that he caught the look in her eyes and for a moment he wanted to lean in and kiss her, but he didn't and settled into a pillow.

"You're really a kind man under all that bluster," she said after drinking down some tea. "Especially given what happened at Holy Rollers the other morning. It's been the elephant in the room every time you and I have been together. I don't know why we can't seem to talk about it."

He wasn't good at handling compliments of any kind. One of his teachers in high school had taught him to simply thank the person and let it go, but still, he never could get used to it.

"Don't tell anyone that I can be a nice guy or they won't respect my mad-dog authority anymore. What happened at Holy Rollers?"

Her forehead furrowed. "I, um… We, um… That's when it came out about your connection with Lily."

"Oh, that." He wasn't angry anymore, not since he'd seen Coco shivering and thought about her with hypothermia. Now, that was serious. Everything else could be dealt with.

She stared at him hard. "*Oh, that?* This is your opportunity to lay into me. Why aren't you?"

"Lay into you for what?"

"Don't pretend that everyone in town isn't talking about you being Lily's dad."

"I *might* be her dad. We don't know that for sure. There's a good possibility Dani might be lying."

"Is that what everybody is saying? That you *might* be her dad?"

He sipped on his own cup of hot tea that he'd picked up from the nightstand and fought off the last remnants of irritation still swelling below the surface. He was no longer angry at Coco, but rather angry with this darn town and how the people in it loved to spread gossip.

"No. They're saying that I *am* Lily's father. Cindy Whipple even knew that Dani is Lily's mom."

"I can explain," she said, her face contorted in a deep frown. He didn't like seeing her look so sad, not on his account.

"I'm more worried about you getting warm again than how the gossip got started. Besides, folks were bound to find out sooner or later, anyway."

"Yeah, but this was way sooner than either one of us had anticipated."

"More tea?" he asked, not wanting to talk about it anymore. He would have to learn how to deal with it on his own terms, and so would she, for that matter. This affected both of them as long as he was living in her spare room.

"No, thanks," she told him. "I still have some."

He went into the kitchen, bringing his things along with him, hanging his coat out on the hook along with his hat. The way he had it figured, the cow had already left the barn. No putting her back now.

He made himself another cup of tea. Checked his text messages—nothing that Nash wasn't already handling—and went back and sat on the bed next to Coco. Color had returned to her face, and she had pushed the blanket down to her chest.

"Where's Lily?" he asked, missing the sweet little darling.

"She's with Drew and her parents. Turns out her parents love babies as much as Drew does, so getting Lily away from them will be a challenge. They'd like to move her right in."

"They're doing me a tremendous favor, and I'm grateful. So are you. Thanks again."

"But aren't you angry about all of this?"

He turned so he could see her, one leg bent for comfort. "I have to admit, there were moments in the last couple of days when I was seeing red, but I'm okay with it now, if you are."

She put her cup down on the old trunk she used as a nightstand on her side of the bed and stared at him, obviously building up the courage to say something he probably didn't want to hear.

"I'd like to explain what happened. It was my fault... Russ and I had a bit of a miscommunication when I told him what was going on. He thought I said..."

He held up a hand. "You don't have to go any further. It wasn't your fault. I know exactly what happened and why."

Jet had forgotten the bond Coco still had with Russ. He never thought she would tell Russ so soon about the details of Jet's recent discovery. Jet knew couples told each other everything, but he simply didn't realize the speed with which "everything" flowed.

Well, maybe not everything. He had a hunch, from the way Coco talked about her relationship with Russ, that she didn't know about the blonde in Jackson Hole, but Russ seemed to know everything about Coco. She was more like an open book, whereas Russ only told her what she needed to know.

Jet decided he would have to keep that in mind while they were still living together. He could understand why Coco liked to keep the channels of communication open with Russ, and Russ was apparently like a conduit to the folks in town, especially when it came to gossip about the sheriff, who he seemed to dislike almost as much as his rival, Mayor Sally Hickman, one of Jet's few personal friends.

"In Russ's defense, I wasn't as clear as I should have been."

"You should know up front, in my view, there is no defense for Russ Knightly's actions. I'm not fond of the man, and I'm sure the feeling is mutual. If that's a problem, I can take Lily and get a room in a hotel."

She didn't respond right away, and Jet braced himself for a negative reply. He thought for sure she'd tell him that it might be better if he did just that.

"That's not necessary. I would like you and Lily to stay. I'm sure this was simply a misunderstanding that Russ and I will sort through. In the meantime, you and Lily will always be welcome to stay right here… not here in my bed, but in my apartment."

He liked her response and how she got all flustered qualifying her invitation. "Hmm. I liked the first offer better, but I'll take the second. Thanks."

She glanced at the clock and threw off her comforter. "Is that the time?"

It was going on six o'clock.

"Yes. Why?"

She slid out of bed and stood, a little shaky at first, but then she put her hands on her hips, looking determined.

"I have a date with Russ that I intend to keep."

"You're kidding, right? Just ten minutes ago you were near death."

"Ten minutes ago I thought you were mad at me."

"I didn't say I wasn't. Exactly."

"Well, then, how about I simply move forward with my plans?"

"Are you saying you weren't as cold as I thought

you were? That you were playing me to keep me from giving you a piece of my mind?"

"And what piece was that?"

"The angry piece."

"Didn't we just cover that? Keep that anger for your criminals and speeders and whoever else you have to arrest. Right now I need to get dressed before Drew brings Lily back."

"And when will that be?"

The doorbell rang. "That's probably her. Or it could be that Russ is early."

"I can't believe you're still going out with that guy."

"In case you didn't notice, Russ is my boyfriend."

"You mean the man who betrayed your trust? That man is your boyfriend?"

"It was a mistake, I'm sure. The Knightlys have done a lot for this town and for my brother. I refuse to believe Russ would purposely do anything that might hurt me or you or an innocent baby. Russ is a hero."

"By whose standards?"

"Just about everyone's in this town, including mine."

Jet had heard about Russ saving those trapped mustangs in the mountains, but he'd also heard that it was in fact Coco's brother, Carson, who got those horses out. Apparently, for some reason, Carson had given all the credit to Russ, who couldn't even make it up the mountain.

But the sheriff couldn't validate that rumor because Carson wasn't the type of guy to blow his own horn, nor was he the kind of guy who would try to undermine someone else's glory.

She went to take a step and staggered.

He bolted out of the bed and gathered her up in his arms. She willingly went along with it.

"Jet, I..." she began, then stopped.

This time when he looked into her eyes he saw something more than mere gratitude. He saw affection, and as soon as he recognized it, she pulled back.

"It's okay. I understand," he said. "But you're in no shape to go anywhere or do anything. In fact, you've been doing too much. Maybe you should take a break for tonight. I'll care for Lily and those remaining critters downstairs. You get some rest. There's nothing pressing me to go back into work. I can stay right here."

He gently put her down on the bed and covered her up again, but with fewer blankets this time.

She didn't argue.

"I'd like that," she told him, smiling.

The thing about it was, whenever she smiled at him his whole world lit up. He had it bad for Doctor Coco Grant, who just happened to be in love with another man. That was the story of his life. Why should this woman, this situation, be any different?

The doorbell rang again and Jet went to answer it. He assumed it was Drew. He hadn't seen Lily all day, and found that he missed the little darlin'. He knew he shouldn't allow himself to get attached to her or to Coco, but he couldn't help it.

"But what do I tell Russ?" Coco shouted from the

bedroom, fracturing Jet's pleasant thoughts. Just the mention of Russ's name soured his stomach.

"That you're sick," he shouted back over his shoulder as he opened the apartment door.

"This will be the third date I've broken with him. He's going to think I'm avoiding him."

Jet liked that scenario, but he didn't want to make waves between himself and Coco. He descended the stairs and swung open the door as he quickly turned back to say, "I'm sure Russ will understand."

"Understand what?" Russ asked, standing in the doorway, carrying a dozen red roses and a bottle of wine.

"That Coco isn't feeling up to going out with you tonight."

"What are you, her doctor now?" Russ gave Jet a dismissive look, then brushed past him and hustled upstairs.

Jet followed close behind the arrogant sneak, wishing he would simply go away, but knowing the man was probably here to stay.

"Hey, babe, where are you?" Russ shouted while standing in the living room. Jet walked up next to him and gathered up his things off the hook next to the door.

"In here." Coco's voice echoed through the apartment. She sounded as if she was feeling much better. Still, Jet wanted to make sure. He trailed Russ back to Coco's bedroom.

As soon as he saw the blissful look on her face

when she saw Russ, Jet knew he was the odd man out in this situation.

Russ entered the bedroom. "Oh, babe. We've got all night to make you well again," he said, shutting the door in Jet's face.

Chapter Eight

"You're early," Coco said as Russ sat down on the bed next to her.

"What are you doing under the covers?" he asked.

"I got a little too much cold weather and Jet… I'm going to have to break our date tonight. Again. I know you had a fund-raiser for us to attend, but I can't go."

"No worries. The fund-raiser was canceled because of the weather. They're forecasting more snow. We can order in and watch a movie, or…" He leaned over to kiss her and for the very first time, she pulled away from his kiss.

"I'm sorry, I really don't feel well, and I don't want you to catch anything. But maybe if I eat something, I might feel better. I'm in the mood for some hot soup from Sammy's. What about you?"

"I'm in the mood, all right, but it's not for soup." He crawled up on the bed after he put the roses and the wine down on the trunk. As strange as it now seemed, all she could think of was how much she didn't want him to be there.

She wanted Jet, not Russ.

She tried to laugh off his advance. "I am sorry, but we need to wait on this. I want to be at my best."

He stared at her for a moment and then moved away. "Okay. I understand. I'll order soup for you, and some ribs for me. We'll have a picnic in bed."

Truth be told, she didn't want Russ in her bed, or in her apartment, for that matter. And she especially didn't want him there with Jet in the other room.

The doorbell rang again. A second later she heard Drew's voice.

"I haven't seen Lily since this morning. Do you think you could ask Drew to bring her in here?" Coco asked, hoping he would at least do that much. What if Jet was going out for the evening?

"Babe, I haven't seen *you* for way too long. Can't we have some time to ourselves?"

Coco knew he was right. They needed their own time alone. To talk about their relationship and about what had happened at Holy Rollers when he'd revealed the news about the sheriff.

She'd reacted to what Russ had done more strongly than she would have thought possible...but still, they needed to discuss it. Yet, the more she heard Drew and Jet laughing in the other room, the more she wanted to be out there, instead of in the bedroom with Russ.

She slipped out of bed. Russ got up and said, "I thought you didn't feel well."

"I don't, but I want to see Lily."

She entered the living room just as Jet left.

"Where's the sheriff going?" she asked Drew, who

stood, holding Lily comfortably in a sling resting on her chest.

"He went over to the station. I have a date with Nash, and my parents have a dinner party to go to at my cousin's house, so if you want them to take Lily along, they will, but I thought I should ask you first."

"Yes!" Russ said without hesitation, leaning on the bedroom doorjamb.

Coco looked at Russ. "Um, I haven't spent any time with Lily since this morning and I'd love for us to keep her right here."

"But Sheriff Wilson said that you and Mr. Knightly might want to be alone," Drew countered.

"And we do," Russ chimed in, grinning.

"Actually, what Mr. Knightly really means is that he and I would be happy to have some alone time with Lily."

"You would?" Drew asked Russ. "Even now, when you know that Lily might be Sheriff Wilson's daughter? Wow! You *are* a great man. What other guy would want to do that? I wasn't going to vote for you, but now that I know you're so nice, I may change my mind."

Russ smiled and Coco knew Drew had caught him by complete surprise. He needed every vote that he could get. "Certainly I want to spend time with the sweetheart. Little Millie means the world to me."

"Lily," Drew corrected.

"That's what I said. Lily."

Then he went over and tried to take a sleeping Lily from Drew, who wouldn't let him. "I fed her about a half hour ago and finally got her to sleep. We shouldn't wake her up just yet. She'll be mad."

"Let's put her in her bassinet, Drew. It's on the floor in my bedroom. Please pick it up and put it in the middle of the bed before you put her down. Thanks so much."

"You got it," Drew said cheerily and went off to take care of Lily.

"Did you mean that? That you do want to spend time with Lily?"

Russ busied himself playing with his phone. "Sure, but I just got a text from Ben Cartwright and he has some news that he can only tell me in person. So I have to jump, babe." Ben was Russ's campaign manager and best friend. The two of them were like brothers.

Russ gave Coco one of those air kisses and rushed for the door. "Tell you what, babe. You call me when you're free for a real date. I have a lot going on, and this, whatever *this* is, can't work right now. Once the campaign is over and I'm the mayor, things will calm down, but for the time being, with the sheriff moving in with you, it doesn't look too good. Besides, I don't like the guy and I'm not crazy that you asked him to move in without asking me first. You know how this town is. The rumors are already flying about you and the sheriff having an affair."

Wait. She couldn't believe that he just told her she needed his permission to ask someone to stay in her own apartment. She wanted to tell him what she thought of his small-minded opinion, but Drew was close by in the other room.

Instead, she held back and said, "You know none of those rumors are true."

"I know and you know the truth, but the townsfolk only know what they perceive to be the truth. So until it's just you and me again, we should cool it."

His words swirled around in her head until she landed on a thought that caused her irritation to escalate.

"Are you breaking up with me?"

"Absolutely not, but you can't have it both ways. It's either him or me. This town and clearly this apartment aren't big enough for the both of us. I gotta run."

And with that, he left, slamming the door behind him. Lily immediately woke up and had no problem wailing her disgust at Russ Knightly's ultimatum.

IT HAD BEEN more than three days since Russ had walked out and Coco still didn't know exactly how she felt about the situation.

She'd started to call him a couple of times, to try to sort out the situation between them, but then never went through with the call. Something always stopped her. She didn't like ultimatums and she especially didn't like Russ's temper…a side of him she'd never seen before, and hoped to never see again.

Her feelings for Russ were all jumbled up, she knew that much, so rather than make any sort of decision about their relationship, she decided to let it be.

In the meantime, she, Jet, Lily, Punky and the critters that needed homes who still lived in her clinic had all become good friends. She'd been too busy during the day at the clinic to spend much time with anyone. On the days when he could, Jet volunteered to take Lily with him, assuring Coco that her instincts about the sheriff were good. He'd make a fine dad. So it was the evenings when she and Jet were able to spend time together with not only Lily, but the entire group of friends from downstairs.

On her ranch rounds she'd managed to get the piglet adopted by Travis Granger, and the puppy, Mister Wiggles, seemed to love his new home with old Mr. McGregor, who'd been looking for a companion pet. That left Tortie the tortoise, and the two kittens, Garth and Reba, who rolled around on the kitchen floor while Jet tried his best not to step on a tail or a paw as he finished frying the chicken. He'd already whipped up a pot of Idaho's finest Yukon Gold potatoes along with boiling some frozen sweet corn. Tortie wanted nothing to do with the kittens and instead made his way back and forth through the apartment, trying to find a good hiding place.

Coco had put together a mixed green salad about an hour earlier, before Lily had needed a bottle and a diaper change.

Garth and Reba no longer lived down in the clinic once Coco closed up shop for the day. She couldn't seem to get them or Tortie adopted out, despite the cute posts she'd left on Cindy Whipple's community bulletin board in her store. Coco took the critters up to the apartment, and of course, just like Lily, into her heart, a vice she knew she needed to work on.

"Sorry about these little guys having to be with us

at night, but I just don't have the heart to leave them down in their cages. They need to be around people."

The problem was, the more time she spent with Jet, the more he made inroads into her heart, as well. Ever since Russ had left her place, she found she hadn't really given him much thought…which told her a lot about her own emotions.

How could she have gone from thinking Russ Knightly was the man she wanted to marry, the man she loved, to having feelings for Jet Wilson, a man who annoyed her so much? A man who did everything by the book…or at least he used to.

She couldn't figure out how one tiny baby could have changed him so quickly.

Jet, who had told her that he wasn't used to kittens or puppies or critters of any kind, had apparently decided to simply go along with all of it.

And the thing that truly set her mind spinning was that he seemed to enjoy coming home to the chaos.

"Not a problem," he'd told her as the kittens ran between his feet. "I'm sure you'll find permanent homes for them soon."

"I'm trying, but finding somewhere for two kittens at once can be a challenge. I don't want to break them up. They love each other and it would be traumatic for them to be separated. And finding a home for a tortoise is next to impossible, although the 4-H Club might have a few members who may be interested. Tortie certainly qualifies as an interesting pet."

"I don't know why I didn't think of this before, but you can petition the town council to change the law.

They can make it so if any kind of livestock is abandoned on your doorstep, you have a predetermined length of time to find homes for them outside city limits. That way, you can avoid all the fines."

"That's a great idea. Sounds like a win-win."

Just then, the kittens and Punky ran past Coco. Barking ensued, startling Lily, who began to wail in Coco's arms. Coco gently bounced her, telling her that everything was all right. It didn't take long for Lily to begin to settle again, almost as if she was beginning to adjust to Coco's voice, and her touch. Coco tried not to think about Lily's future, and instead concentrated on giving her all the love she could right now. She'd learned to move past her emotions when it came to all the animals that had been left on her doorstep, but doing the same for Lily seemed impossible. Whatever happened, she knew she was headed for heartache, but she couldn't help herself. She'd fallen in love with baby Lily and all her nuances. Especially the way she looked up at Coco, eyes bright, little fists punching the air, and the sweetest of smiles creasing her delicate lips whenever Coco sang to her.

Not long ago, she could never have imagined that she'd be falling for such a darling baby or that Sheriff Jet Wilson would be standing in her kitchen, cooking up dinner in the midst of so much noise and traffic. But there he was, flannel shirtsleeves rolled up, well-worn, torn jeans hitting his bare feet, thick dark hair tousled—a man looking as though he was enjoying himself.

She'd never known a man who seemed more at

home with complete bedlam going on around him than Jet Wilson. Even her dad, who loved to help out in the kitchen like Jet, had his limits.

This man broke all the rules, and she couldn't help but like it...a lot.

"Dinner smells wonderful," Coco said as she stood in the kitchen doorway, trying to soothe Lily to sleep.

"I hope it tastes as good as it smells," Jet said over the mayhem all around him. "What's up with Lily?"

"She's just tired and doesn't want to give up the fight."

The kittens nudged Coco's legs, wanting her affection.

"Hey, guys," Jet said. "Let's play in your pen." He then picked up the two squirming kittens and put them down in their plastic snap-together toddler play yard in the middle of the living room, along with Punky, who tried his best to wiggle from Jet's strong hands. Kendra Myers had given the play yard to Coco for Lily, but it turned out to be perfect for the menagerie and all their toys.

Soon Punky and the kittens attacked each other affectionately, rolling around in friendly playful bliss, all making sweet guttural noises.

"Where'd you learn to cook?" Coco whispered once Lily began closing her eyes and soothing herself as she sucked on her closed fist.

"I picked up a love of cooking from one of the families I lived with, the Garcias," Jet told her as he served them dinner, bringing the steaming plates over to the dining table. "Mr. Garcia did all the cooking and I'd lend a hand. I loved it. Then he lost his job and they had to move to another town and couldn't take me. I was with them for almost two years."

"That must have been tough to lose all of that."

"I think that one hurt me the most, but I toughed it out. I was sixteen and used to moving around by then."

"Still, the disappointment had to stick with you. You were only a kid."

"Well, shortly after that I went to live with my mom. If we hadn't fought so much, and I hadn't been so rebellious, it probably would have been a decent time in my life. Sometimes I just can't tell when I have it good."

Like now, she thought, but couldn't say it out loud. There was always an edge to Jet Wilson, like he couldn't completely relax even when he had no reason not to. It seemed to Coco as if the man was always anticipating the rug slipping out from under his feet. She wished for once, for one night even, that he could find peace within himself. But from what she'd seen so far, it seemed impossible.

Still, she liked to think her place gave him some solace for the time being.

He walked over to Coco while holding tongs in one hand and a yellow dishtowel draped over his shoulder, peeking in at Lily. "She's sound asleep."

"Perfect timing. I'll put her down," Coco murmured, as she moved into the living room, the menagerie beginning to tire as they curled up on each other for a nap. The sight of those happy kittens, along with

Punky, feeling safe and comfy pulled at Coco's heart-strings. But she wasn't going to focus on all that now.

Coco just wanted to get Lily down as soon as possible. Once she was in dreamland, the sweet baby could sleep through almost anything, but getting her to fall asleep had always been the challenge. She smiled down at the little girl, now snoring softly.

Coco put Lily on the sofa, rolled up a pink receiving blanket and placed it next to her. Not that Lily could possibly tumble off, but Coco would never be too careful when it came to Lily's safety.

With Lily secure, Coco walked back to the kitchen. "Can I do anything?"

She caught Jet's intense gaze as he turned to her. For a brief moment, she wanted to melt into his arms and have him hold her close, feel his strong body embracing hers, knowing she would feel safe and comforted, too. She could tell he was feeling some of the same emotions…as if he wanted to kiss her. He leaned in.

But she took a step back. "Jet, I…"

He stood up straight again and nodded toward the dining room. "Everything is done and on the table. Let's eat before Lily wakes up."

Coco didn't argue as Jet poured each of them a glass of red wine. "By the way, Doc Starr said I should have the results of that DNA test any day now."

The back of Coco's neck tightened as she took a seat across from him at the table. "Are you nervous?"

"I'd like everything settled," he said, avoiding her glance and taking a few sips of wine.

"So it doesn't bother you that you may have to give up Lily?"

"I wouldn't say that, exactly."

He poked two pieces of chicken with a fork and carefully placed them on his plate. She searched his face for any tells that this whole subject tortured his soul, but she didn't see any emotion at all.

"What if she's yours? Will you keep her?"

He finally looked at her, his face solemn, guarding any emotion. "No matter what the outcome, I'll do what's best for Lily."

"I don't know what that means."

He put his fork down and stared into her eyes. "It means that I can't allow my feelings to get the best of me. At this point, I have no idea whether or not I'm Lily's father. If I am, then my life may have to change. If I'm not, there are different options for her that can happen." His face softened as he quickly peered over at Lily, then focused again on Coco. "I've had years of practice at shoring up what I'm feeling. This time it's especially difficult because of...well, because of you. You've shown Lily and me nothing but kindness and support, and we're both thankful for that. Problem is, I'm in law enforcement, and as such, I can't allow my emotions to sway me one way or the other. I hope you can understand that."

Coco's throat tightened as tears burned the corners of her eyes. She could tell that Jet was trying his best to keep his distance until he knew the truth. He certainly didn't need her to get all mushy on him by crying.

"I understand," Coco said, holding back her tears.

She drank down some of the delicious wine with the cherry undertones. It was the bottle that Russ had brought over the other night, but never got a chance to open. She knew he wouldn't like the idea of the sheriff drinking a bottle of wine intended for himself and Coco, but she was in a feisty mood ever since Russ had given her his ultimatum.

"This looks great. Almost as good as my mom's cooking, which you're going to love tomorrow night."

Every Sunday, Coco's parents hosted a family dinner that also included several guests. Coco had invited Jet just that morning, before they both went off to work.

"Looking forward to it," he said, breaking into a grin. Still, Coco detected apprehension. "But shouldn't it be Russ going to a traditional Sunday dinner with the Grant family?"

"Actually, there's something I should tell you about my relationship with Russ," she began.

Just then, her phone chirped, and as if he knew she'd been talking about him, Russ's picture appeared on her screen.

She stared in disbelief. Eventually, Russ had relented and finally called her. She didn't know how to react, how she felt, if she, in fact, felt anything at all for him anymore.

"Aren't you going to answer that?" Jet asked, breaking her trance.

"No," she told him with conviction. "This is our time, and I don't want anything or anyone getting in the way of that."

Jet held up his glass. "To us."

"To us," she echoed, clinking his glass, and for the next couple of hours, she and Jet enjoyed their dinner and each other with absolutely no distractions.

COCO AGREED TO meet Russ at the pancake breakfast over at St. Paul's hall, and had dressed for the occasion in a gray sweater dress and her best lace-up black boots. She'd even applied the full spectrum of makeup, including a shiny pink lipstick. Lily had been cooperative that morning, and not only allowed her a complete shower, but also didn't make one peep while she dressed. It was a miracle of sorts, so Coco was ready for whatever came her way.

Whatever the result, she and Russ needed to come to terms.

This was the third year for the pancake event, which was held around Thanksgiving. The sweet breakfast was a fund-raiser for Spuds and Turkeys Across Idaho. Each year, various places of worship of all religions would hold a pancake breakfast and the money would be pooled to buy turkeys and a sack of Idaho potatoes for anyone who couldn't afford to put Thanksgiving dinner on their table. Last year, the breakfasts brought in over two hundred thousand dollars. This year, they expected to reach over three hundred thousand dollars, which amounted to one heck of a lot of spuds and turkeys.

"This isn't exactly conducive to us having a conversation," Coco said to Russ as she poured batter onto one of several hot pancake griddles. She hadn't been planning to pour batter this year, but somehow had gotten talked into it by her cousin, Father Beau, who was also one of the cooks, along with Doc Granger, the only pediatric dentist in town, and Milo Gump, Amanda's husband and owner of Belly Up Tavern, along with Spud Drive-In. Several other town residents helped prepare the batter, and kept up with cooking the sides, and plating the food. It was a group effort of mega proportions that the good people of Briggs loved to participate in each year. Coco's entire family had already been served and were seated somewhere inside the hall. She had intended to sit with them, until Father Beau along with Russ had commandeered her.

The hall was meant to hold over two hundred people, and from what Coco could tell, at least two hundred and fifty had squeezed inside, with another hundred or so braving the cold to stand in line outside. For fifteen dollars, each person received a full stack of pancakes, sausage, bacon, hash browns and all the coffee, tea or milk they could drink. Kids five and under ate for free, which always brought out most of the young families in town and in the surrounding ranch community.

The batter was donated, along with all of the sides; so 90 percent of that fifteen dollars went to buy the turkeys and potatoes for the less fortunate.

Coco normally loved to volunteer her time to help, but this year, standing in Russ's shadow wasn't very much fun. He was supposed to be handing out the plated pancakes, which was simple enough, but instead he seemed more interested in securing endorsements from the last remaining uncommitted holdouts in town, which slowed everything down.

"What's to talk about?" Russ told her under his breath while wearing a fake smile for everyone he passed a plate to. He looked his usual handsome self in a crisp white shirt, sleeves rolled up like he was working hard in the kitchen, black dress pants and black spit-shined, handmade cowboy boots. "I was wrong. You were right. Besides, everybody in town knows you and I are a couple, and that Sheriff Wilson and his baby are simply a temporary inconvenience."

Coco spoke with her back to the hall filled with people, facing the griddles and a makeshift blue cloth wall behind them. "They aren't an inconvenience at all, and we don't know if Lily is the sheriff's baby. The DNA test hasn't come in yet."

"Oh, please," Russ whispered, still maintaining his smile. "As if there's even a question. He's just shirking his responsibility and trying to hone in on the good thing we've got going on. It's as clear as the pretty little nose on your face. He's making a play for you. Everybody in town knows it. You seem to think it's all about Lily. Believe me, babe, he's playing you."

She resented his calling her *babe*. As if they were still in a relationship, which they most certainly were not.

Coco turned to correct what Russ had said, just as he handed Marty Bean and his family plates filled with pancakes. Marty's dad and Coco's went way back, having served in Vietnam together. "Remember, a vote for Russ Knightly is a vote for a brighter future." He leaned in closer to Marty. "Plus, I can help expedite those permits for the expansion you want to make to Moo's Creamery."

Moo's was the family-owned ice-cream parlor in town. Marty wanted to expand it into a chocolateria as well, and was having a few problems getting his permits approved, but if Coco knew anything about Marty, he was completely against insider favors of any kind.

Marty and his family smiled and kept right on walking toward Mayor Sally Hickman's stand. She and a few of her supporters were serving up the sides. Coco knew for a fact that Marty and his family preferred the incumbent mayor, and from what Russ had just told him, there would be no doubt who Marty and his family would be voting for.

Coco switched back to her griddle and poured out more batter. "Not only did you just alienate the entire Bean family, but I believe you just referred to *us* as in a couple."

"Marty is a businessman. He'll come around. And I would think you'd be happy that I refer to you as my girl, considering the messy circumstances."

Coco flipped a dozen pancakes that were now bubbling on her griddle, desperately trying to control the anger that was building inside her. That anger only intensified when Russ slid his arm around her waist and pulled her in close, as if everything was fine between them.

She instantly shifted away.

Fortunately for Russ no one was paying attention.

He and the other volunteers had set out enough plates with pancakes that everyone just took a plate and continued down the row.

She leaned into him so that he was the only one who could hear what she had to say. "Here's the thing. I'm not *your girl* or *your babe*. Nor have I ever really been *your girl*. We dated briefly and that's it."

"You're overreacting to what I'm saying. Let's wait until later to talk about this, when we're not so in public. I can't afford any more gossip when it comes to our relationship. The townsfolk need to believe we're solid."

She wanted to yell it out, but she restrained herself. "Solid? Is that why you asked me here? So everyone thinks we're still a couple? You're the one who gave me an ultimatum and told me I had to choose between you and Sheriff Wilson."

His face softened as a smile stretched his tight, thin lips. "I was wrong to put you in that position and I'm sorry. But you have to understand where I'm coming from. It doesn't look good that my girl is sharing her apartment with another man. It's bad for my image."

"Your image?"

"Yes. I'm running for mayor against an incumbent who seems to have the morals of a saint. I can't have anyone associated with me who isn't held to those same high standards." He spoke under his breath. A tone so low she could barely hear him with all the loud voices and laughter bouncing off the walls.

"Let me get this straight. You're worried that I

might lose the election for you because I've taken in a helpless baby and Sheriff Wilson, who needed a place to stay while his apartment is being repaired. Since when is that immoral?"

He greeted a few more people, and gave them his vote-for-me pitch while Coco waited for an answer. After the folks walked on past, he turned his attention back to Coco, still wearing a charming smile.

"You're twisting what I'm saying," he whispered, his voice sounding sharp and curt.

That was the last straw.

"I'm not twisting anything except maybe this so-called relationship. I'm hereby announcing that I'm breaking up with you," she said and handed him the spatula as she peeled off the white apron she'd slipped on earlier.

"You can't be serious."

"As serious as a war."

"Don't do this. The election is only a couple days away. You know how much it means to me and how many great things I have planned for this town, and for you, for that matter. It will no longer be illegal for you to take in abandoned livestock within city limits. That one change will be a benefit to you and to those unfortunate animals. If you have any feelings left for me at all, you won't make this public. Not now. Not when your brother, Carson, is set to officially endorse me during this breakfast."

"I don't need you to change the law for me. I can petition the town council myself. You don't care one bit for those abandoned animals. You only care about winning at any cost."

Their relationship suddenly became crystal clear. It was all about getting the town hero, Carson's endorsement. What a fool she'd been.

"Let's not jump to any conclusions. Our relationship shouldn't be a factor in this election. It's not fair to the good people of Briggs."

Okay. He had a point. She didn't want to be personally responsible for changing anyone's vote. This was between her and Russ. No one else needed to know the truth about their nonrelationship until after the election.

"Fine. I won't tell anyone. At least not yet. But make no mistake, this thing we had is over." She'd whispered it with a great big smile on her face, as if she was telling him a sweet story. Then she kissed him on the cheek, put her apron down on the table next to the griddle and made her way to the door. Feeling as though she'd finally taken the blinders off and the road ahead of her was now clear.

THE LAST TIME Jet had been to the Grant ranch, their horse barn had been on fire. It had been one of those nights he'd rather forget, especially the sounds of the horses that were trapped inside. Fortunately, all the horses had made it out in time, and the brand-new barn that now stood directly in front of him was a sight to behold.

Jet hadn't liked to talk about the fire much, probably because it gave him his own nightmares. One of the families he'd lived with had lost everything when their roof had caught on fire on Christmas Eve from hot ash in the fireplace. Everyone was safe in the end, but all their things, including the gifts under the tree, went up in flames. In the aftermath, Jet had lost one of his first families. They were the only ones who had filed to adopt him, but after the fire, they couldn't afford to keep him. It had been his first real disappointment in a long line of many to come.

Never had he reflected on his life so much as he had since Lily arrived. And even now, being around her only reminded him of what her future would be like if she wasn't his baby.

Even if she were his baby, how could he possibly be an attentive father with his particular job? If something happened to him, she'd end up in foster care. Just because Briggs was an easygoing town, with virtually no crime, didn't mean someone couldn't come in and put his and someone else's life in jeopardy. Anything was possible.

"That's some great barn," Jet told Coco as they leisurely strolled toward it after dinner. Jet carried Lily in a sling as she slept all warm and cozy up against his chest, while little Punky followed on a red leash. It was a clear night with a full moon bright in a cloudless sky, a night without any wind to chill the already crisp air. The Teton Mountain Range loomed in the distance, reminding Jet how much he loved this valley.

"It can hold twenty-five horses, and was built to the strictest fire codes. Nothing short of cannon fire can bring it down now. I still can't believe it sometimes. Half the town pitched in both with the supplies and with muscle thanks to Jake Scott putting out the word. He really came through for our family and I'm so proud to have him as a brother-in-law. He's a true hero in my book."

"In anyone's book, to be sure."

"That barn serves as a constant reminder of how quickly life can change in a heartbeat."

Lily squirmed against his chest, tiny knees and elbows poking at him. "I know something about life-changing moments."

"Unfortunately so does Lily. Whatever happens to her, I feel lucky that she was dropped off on my doorstep and I've been able to be part of her life."

Almost on instinct, he took Coco's hand in his. "I am, too. You've been wonderful to both of us. Thank you for that."

They were inside the warmth of the dimly lit barn now. A few of the horses nickered and scraped the bottom of their stalls. The familiar smells that Jet actually liked filled his head with some good memories and some not-so-good memories. Regardless, they made up the fabric of his life, and this night only added to it.

"My pleasure. I'd do it again in a heartbeat."

He turned to her. "I only hope Lily can grow up with all the love I felt around your dinner table tonight. Your parents are a delight, and the banter between Carson, his wife, Zoe, and your sisters, Callie, Kayla and Kenzie, is a riot. Not to mention the seemingly tight friendship between their spouses. I don't think I've ever witnessed anything like it. Thank you for inviting me. But again, shouldn't it have been Russ?"

"That's what I wanted to talk to you about, away from my family. I promised Russ I wouldn't tell anyone until after the election, even though I rarely keep anything from my family. Still, I thought I should tell you first. I broke up with Russ today."

Jet could hardly believe what she'd just said. "Is this for good? I mean, are you sure? He might be the new mayor and you'd be, well, maybe one day, be the town's first lady."

Although he doubted that Russ could settle for any one woman, even someone as truly wonderful as Coco Grant. The man was a complete fool to let her go.

"It's not a title that suits me."

"What does suit you?"

"Doctor Coco Grant, the woman dating Sheriff Jet Wilson."

He let out the breath he'd been holding. "Are you sure about that?"

"Been sure for a while now…that is, if you'll consider…"

But before she could utter another word, he leaned in, raked his hands through her thick hair and kissed her, hard, wanting her to know how much he'd been wanting her since that first night they'd spent together on her bed.

Of course, Lily picked that exact moment to start

squirming and then let out one of her ear-shattering wails that scared some of the horses. Soon the entire barn erupted with angry whinnies that only grew louder with a crying baby.

"Let's pick this up later," Jet told her.

"Uh-huh," she whispered as they held hands and quickly walked back to the house.

Chapter Nine

The very next night, despite the fact that Coco had promised Russ that she would keep their breakup a secret, Jet decided to ask Coco out on a proper date. He wasn't planning on announcing anything to anyone, nor was he planning on kissing her in public. However, he thought the breakup was cause for a celebration away from Lily where they might get some time alone. And if anything sparked after that, they'd just have to find somewhere private to ignite that fire.

Drew was babysitting at Coco's place where Deputy Sheriff Nash Young was planning to stop by, according to Drew, who had a crush on Nash a mile wide.

In truth, all Jet wanted was a relaxing meal that neither he nor Coco had to cook and that wouldn't be interrupted by a needy baby…not that he in the least bit minded taking care of Lily. He found that he truly enjoyed it, but tonight was all about spending time with Coco. He even wore a suit for the occasion.

Hot Tomato, one of the oldest and the only upscale restaurant in Briggs, was owned by two generations of the Salerno family. Everyone in the family worked or helped in the restaurant, including little Mary Salerno, who couldn't be more than ten or eleven years old. She sometimes greeted the patrons as they arrived.

Tonight was no exception. Coco and Jet had decided they would meet each other at the restaurant due to their schedules. They figured since they were already living together temporarily no one would be the wiser.

"Good evening and welcome to Hot Tomato," Mary told Jet as he walked through the front door. Mary wore a pretty hunter green velvet dress, white tights, black patent shoes and a matching green satin bow in her long dark hair, which was neatly parted on her right side.

She reminded Jet of what Lily might look like when she was Mary's age, and it made him wonder if he would still be a part of Lily's life by then. Funny thing was, for the first time in his entire life, he allowed himself to hope for something that was a long way off, and it scared him.

He pushed that thought out of his head. Tonight was all about Coco and he didn't want anything to get in the way of that. He was getting ready to enter a relationship with a woman who was unlike anyone he'd ever dated before, a woman he'd lusted over for months, a woman who was by far the kindest person he'd ever known.

For one thing, she had roots, real roots that bore down deep into Briggs, and he liked that concept.

He'd grown weary of living a "temporary" life where he couldn't or wouldn't commit to anything or anyone for the long term. Even his position of sheriff in Briggs was subject to the pleasure or displeasure of the mayor, and if Russ won the election, Jet's job could end on Russ's first day.

"So nice to see you, Mary. That's a very pretty dress."

"Thank you, Sheriff Wilson," Mary said with a smile. Then she held out her hand, pointing to the podium. "Right this way to check in with the hostess."

Jet followed directions. It was still fairly early, only six thirty, so the restaurant wasn't very busy. He was hoping for a table in the back of the restaurant where he and Coco could have some privacy.

As soon as he checked in with the hostess, Mary's seventeen-year-old sister, with whom he exchanged quick hugs and double kisses, she escorted him to the absolute perfect table where Coco was already seated.

A great big welcoming smile lit up her beautiful face, then she stood and kissed him on each check, Italian style, and he willingly reciprocated.

"I could get used to this real easy-like," he said, wanting to pull her in closer before she backed away from his embrace.

"It's the official Salerno greeting," she told him, her face showing a slight blush.

"We should adopt it."

"Done," she said, chuckling then sitting back down in her wooden chair across from him.

It was the first he'd seen of her alone since they'd

kissed the previous night. Lily had needed immedi-
ate attention after that, and they'd gone back to the
house to feed her. Then they'd given Father Beau, who
had also attended the dinner, a ride to St. Paul's, and
by the time they walked into Coco's apartment, Lily
needed feeding and changing again. Of course, after
all the excitement, Lily wouldn't fall back to sleep,
so Jet stayed up with her until she finally drifted off
around two in the morning, only to wake back up
again at five.

Needless to say he was dog-tired, but nothing was
going to stop this dinner.

"You look beautiful…stunning actually," Jet told
Coco, as his gaze gently caressed her lovely curves.

She'd worn a very low-cut navy blue cocktail dress
that only increased his intense desire for her.

"I haven't worn this dress since a friend's wedding in Boise a couple of years ago. It's a bit risqué
for Briggs."

He wanted to devour her.

"It's perfect," he said, knowing his voice had gone
down an octave. The excitement that rushed through
his body made him wonder if he was going to be able
to get through this dinner without kissing her. He felt
grateful they weren't in a booth sitting side by side,
but instead in chairs directly across from each other.

"You don't look so bad yourself," she said. "I don't
think I've ever seen you in an actual suit."

"That's because I've never owned one until today.
Never had the need."

"You bought a suit for me? For our date?"

"I did." If he were the blushing kind, he knew his face would be bright red.

"Jet Wilson, you do something to amaze me almost every day."

"I hope that's a good thing."

Her full lips stretched into a big smile. "A very good thing."

Just then Mama Salerno, a short, plump, classically Old World–looking woman in her midseventies walked up to the table with an open bottle of wine and two stemmed glasses. "This is a wonderful thing to see you two in my restaurant. Tonight, the wine, she is on me."

Mama Salerno poured two glasses, then gave each of them a hug and double kisses.

"Thank you," both Jet and Coco said almost in unison.

Mama took a couple steps back, holding her hands together just under her ample chest. "So, tell me, how is that baby of yours? I hear she's a little doll. You're gonna have to bring her in so I can bless her. Nothing bad will happen once I bless her. I have the power. It's been passed down to me through the generations. It's the tradition in my family." She held up a hand, waving to indicate a very long time.

"I will," Jet told her to Coco's surprised look. "Anything to keep her safe."

"I always knew you was a good man," Mama Salerno said, squeezing his shoulder. Then she gazed over at Coco. "That Russ Knightly ain't the man for you. Trust me. I know the truth."

Then she turned and strolled back to the kitchen.

"She's right, you know," Jet told Coco. "I have it from a reliable source that Mama is always spot on with her advice."

"Oh, yeah? And who's your source?"

"I can't say or they'll put a curse on me."

"And you believe in curses?"

"Only when they benefit me."

"And this does, I take it."

"One hundred percent."

Coco laughed and Jet's entire world brightened. This night was off to a great start and it could only get better from here on out.

"ARE YOU SURE it's okay that we're in here?" Coco asked as she followed Jet inside the dark police station.

Coco had to admit it was perhaps the craziest place she'd ever made love...not that she had much experience with making love in crazy places. That trophy would probably have to go to her sister Kayla, who was caught kissing Wade Porter when they were budding teens inside the bull pen. Fortunately, Carson had spotted them and pulled them out before their bull was able to charge.

Jet took her hands in his and squeezed. "I'm pretty sure the sheriff said it would be fine," he teased. He gently kissed her while unbuttoning her coat. "Your skin, it's so soft."

She slipped her arms out of her coat, he did the

same with his, allowing both jackets to fall to the floor. "Sheriff, you say the sweetest things."

"I'm sure I'll have more to say, once you're not wearing that dress," he mumbled into her ear as he kissed around the edges of it, which caused her to feel a combination of anticipation and excitement.

She ducked away from him and began to unzip her dress. "Then maybe I should get out of this."

He shrugged out of his suit coat, then started on his tie. "Oh, sweetheart, I can't think of anything better."

Her dress slipped from her, landing by their coats in a puddle of fabric, revealing the deep crimson lace lingerie ensemble she'd picked up that afternoon at Hess's Department Store. She'd decided Jet was more of a hot red man.

"How's this?"

She'd never been so bold in her life, and she liked how it made her feel. Powerful. Seductive. Confident. Happy.

He pulled his shirt off over his head, revealing muscles she'd seen before but couldn't touch. The man was ripped, with a fine dusting of hair on a gorgeous, defined chest.

"You're driving me wild, Coco. You're all I can think about right now."

He swooped in and pulled her tight to him, one hand stroking and cupping her breasts, stirring feelings deep inside her. His kiss was tempting her lips as their tongues gently played the rhythm of desire, causing Coco's knees to go weak.

"Let's just make this easier on both of us," he said

as he picked her up and carried her to the one cell in the back of the jail.

"Am I under arrest?" she asked, playing it up, while wearing a wide grin.

"You sure are. You're my prisoner and I'm locking you in for the night."

"But what have I done?"

"It's what you're about to do," he said, his voice deep and raspy. His eyes had gone almost black, and his skin seemed hot against hers.

He laid her down on the bed in the corner, the bed with the bright blue quilt that the Ladies of Blue Spuds had made last year to perk up the jail. There was even a matching pillowcase. She knew this because she'd contributed a couple squares for the cause. Little had she known that she'd be making love on that very quilt with the sheriff who, at the time, thought the quilt was silly.

She chuckled, warmed by how fast Jet was trying to ditch the rest of his clothes. "But, Sheriff, I'm a good girl."

He quirked his mouth into a smile and quickly slipped out of his dress shoes, pants and briefs, then eased on top of her. Slowly he ran his hands up the sides of her body, then back down again, slipping his thumbs under the corners of her panties. Within moments they were off, along with her bra. She felt free, desired and full of passion for this complicated man.

"You're so beautiful," he said, his hands skimming her body, as if he was exploring every nuance. "I'm so lucky to be here, like this, with you." She arched into his touch, and he gently suckled each breast, caressing her and loving on her.

Her hands roamed over his body, stopping on his manhood until his moans filled her ears with his passion for her.

"Sheriff Wilson, I do believe you've captured my heart."

"Doctor Grant, you've had mine since the first day we met."

"But you were giving me a ticket when we first met."

"I know."

Then his lips came down on hers again, and this time the sensations were too much for her. Emotions ripped through her body as he made it his own, taking her to places she never thought possible.

When he slipped on protection and carefully entered her, she ran her hands up and down his strong back, feeling every muscle as he moved inside her. Feeling him on top of her, inside her, only heightened her ecstasy until they both fell over the edge together in a flurry of delicious whispers that wrapped her in his love.

JET OPENED HIS eyes sometime in the middle of the night, and realized they were both still in the jail cell. Drew would be waiting for them, or at the very least worried about where they'd gotten to.

But first, he had to take a moment to gaze over at Coco, who was fast asleep next to him. She looked even more beautiful when she slept, a pert nose, and beautiful full lips. He gently ran his thumb over her lips. They felt like silk.

She instantly opened her eyes and smiled. Then she turned on her back, exposing those gorgeous breasts of hers, stretching with her arms above her head. He couldn't help himself, he had to taste those breasts again, causing her to giggle.

"Breasts are sensitive, you know. You can't just go kissing them without a chain reaction," she quipped.

He stopped and perched himself up on one elbow so he could stare at her. "What kind of chain reaction?"

"The best kind."

"What if I touched them and caressed each nipple between my fingers?"

She slid down under the covers, letting out a breath. "Only if you want more of what happened last night."

"Is that a promise?" he asked, throwing the covers off her. He hoped they had time for more lovemaking before they had to leave.

As the colorful quilt fell from the bed, he noticed that the cell door was shut. "Wait a minute. When did that door close?"

"What door?"

"The cell door?"

"I don't really know. Why?"

"It has an automatic lock on it."

She leaned over him. "Does that mean we're locked in, Sheriff?"

"It might, if I left my keys in my coat pocket."

She paused and looked at him. "Wait. Is this sexual banter or are you really saying we might be locked in?"

"As much as I would like this to be sexual banter, I'm saying we might be locked in."

She sat up.

Jet sat up.

"Maybe it just looks like we're locked in," she said, almost pleading.

Jet stood, hoping against hope that she was right. The jail suddenly felt freezing cold and he remembered that the temperature in the station was set to lower to sixty-two at night. He reached out for the metal door.

Solid.

He raked a hand through his hair. "Okay, but one of us has a phone, right?"

"Mine's in my purse out on the desk."

"And mine is in my coat pocket along with my keys."

Coco stared at him and then burst out laughing.

"This isn't funny," Jet said, trying to think of how they might get out of there. Looking around he realized there wasn't even a barred window they could scream out of for help.

"Oh, come on, this is very funny. The town sheriff has locked himself and his lover in the one and only jail cell and they can't get out."

Feeling the absurdity of it now, he allowed his barriers to come down and play with the moment. After all, here he was, locked in for the night with Coco Grant. Could life get any better?

"You planned this, didn't you? Getting back at me for all those tickets I've given you?"

Soon he was loving her once again. Nash would just have to let them out later in the morning when he came in.

Still, a pesky notion poked at his thoughts, and he hoped that tomorrow wasn't the morning when the members of the Briggs Historical Restoration Association were scheduled to visit the station. He never could keep those kinds of things straight unless he wrote them down, which he had, on his phone. But his phone wasn't at hand and at the moment, smothering himself in the delights of this fine woman, he had a hard time focusing on anything else.

"THIS PLACE COULD use a complete overhaul," Coco heard a voice say. It sounded like Deputy Sheriff Nash Young, but she couldn't be sure. Her mind was still a little foggy as she slowly opened her eyes. There was the sound of footsteps fast approaching the jail... many sets of footsteps.

"It hasn't been upgraded in well over fifteen years," a woman said. Coco knew the voice, but couldn't quite put a face to it, probably because shock had crept under her skin and threatened to shut her brain down completely.

She stared over at Jet, wide-eyed.

"Oh, boy," Jet said in a whisper, as he leaped off the bed and tugged on his pants. "Cover up."

"You knew about this?"

He handed her the panties and bra from the floor

and she quickly slipped them on under the quilt. Then she pulled the blanket tight up to her chin. A myriad of voices suddenly erupted inside the jail, laughing and talking in fast-paced clips.

"Um, I didn't know when they were stopping by exactly, and I didn't want to needlessly panic you last night. I didn't have my phone to check on the actual date and time."

"So this is better? I'm beyond panicked, I'm mortified!"

Bile crept up her throat. This couldn't be happening.

"I'm so sorry. I never thought—"

"Is that the sheriff?" Coco heard a woman ask.

"And Doctor Grant?" a male voice confirmed with a snicker.

"Well, I'll be doggoned," a husky male voice chided. This time Coco recognized the speaker as Hank Marsh, owner of From The Ground Up Building Supply.

"But, Russ, I thought you and the doctor were a couple?" Sammy Hastings's baritone voice bellowed through the jail. Sammy owned Sammy's Smokehouse and was on several town committees. Darn that Sammy for being so civic-minded.

She winced.

Yep, Coco felt completely and utterly mortified down to her bright pink toenails, which were now sticking out of the bottom of the quilt.

She quickly pulled her feet under the colorful blanket, wishing she could simply disappear…or die. At this point, she'd welcome either one.

"Apparently not anymore," Russ Knightly said loud and clear. "It seems our sheriff has no morals when it comes to wrecking other folks' relationships. What does that say about him doing his job…using the jail as his own private motel?"

Yep, death would be welcomed, Coco mused. Swift and absolute.

"Now, hold on! I can explain," Jet said, standing, wearing his pants but still shirtless. "Nash, can you grab a key and let us out of here, please?" Deputy Sheriff Young didn't move at first, the deer-in-the-headlights phenomenon, Coco assumed. "Nash! The keys!" Jet shouted.

Coco wasn't ready to leave the cell, she realized. If she remembered correctly, her dress was on the other side of the jail…on the floor…with her coat.:. and possibly her shoes.

"Yes. Sure. Keys," the deputy repeated, pulling an overloaded key chain from his pocket, unlocking the door and swinging it open.

Jet bolted out of the cell, and frantically picked up the trail of clothes as he went, trying his best to slip on his shirt and button it. From what Coco could see, everyone followed him, except for Cindy Whipple. She stepped forward with Coco's much-needed dress.

"You might want to put this on, dear," she said, handing Coco her missing clothing. "Huh. There's not much privacy in these cells, is there, dear?" She leaned over to whisper to Coco, "The mister and me did it in a public place once. We were outed by a real busybody, we thought we'd never live it down, but we did. So don't feel bad. These things happen…although, we were smart enough not to get ourselves locked in overnight. But hey, who am I to judge? It still makes me blush, though. Must have been pretty exciting being locked in." Cindy nudged Coco in the arm, as if they were old friends.

"Thanks for bringing in my dress," Coco said without acknowledging Cindy's sisterly comment. She was simply too embarrassed to see the humor at the moment.

"Figured you might be needing it. I put your coat and purse over by the back door if you want to sneak out before all the questions start."

"I can't leave the sheriff to take all the heat. And for the record, I'd broken up with Russ before last night happened."

"He's a brave man, our sheriff. I'm sure he can handle the situation and I'm also sure he wouldn't want you to stick around. Okay, you've broken up with Russ, but his ego must not have gotten the message. He's madder than a hornet caught in a net. No telling who he's gonna sting next."

"He's been humiliated. I can't really blame him."

"I can. He's just a blowhard. Nothing coming out of that mouth of his but wind. I don't think you two were ever meant to be together. You're much too smart for him. Never could see the attraction, but then I never liked the man, myself. Too uppity for his britches. Likes to look down on people, especially if they don't agree with him. The sheriff's a good man, a little too reclusive sometimes, but I suspect that's due to his upbringing. Raising Lily will change all that, believe you me."

"But we don't know for sure if Lily's his baby."

"Either way, I know he'll do the right thing by her, and by you."

"How can I ever thank you?"

"You brought back a memory I had long since forgotten. That's thanks enough in my book. Now skedaddle before Phyllis shows up and starts asking questions you don't want to answer."

Coco gave Cindy a tight hug and left out the back door, feeling as if she'd done something wrong, and secretly happy she had.

"GOT WORD THAT my apartment is livable again," Jet said as he stood in Coco's living room. He'd packed up most of his things, except for the air mattress, while she'd been out with Lily. He hadn't been able to face her all day, so he'd waited until she'd gone out to collect his belongings. He had hoped to have left by the time she returned, but she'd come back sooner than he'd expected. "Under the circumstances I should be moving back into my place."

Coco stood by the open doorway to her apartment, carrying Lily in her car seat.

"Now? Tonight? Shouldn't we talk first?" Coco asked, her voice breaking. He had the distinct feeling that she was about to lose it emotionally, and he didn't want that to happen. He'd made a huge mistake, several to be honest, and he didn't want to compound the issue.

"There's nothing to talk about. I should have never brought you to the station. There was no excuse for it. I'm sorry, and I'm sorry about this morning with the town council and Russ."

"Thanks. I accept your apology, but I'm a grown woman and I knew exactly what I was doing last night. It was an unfortunate accident to have gotten locked in. That wasn't anyone's fault. Now, can we sit down and talk about what this all means? Besides, I wouldn't change anything about last night, and I can't believe that you would, either."

"What happened between us probably shouldn't have. We come from two different worlds. I don't stay in one place for very long. It never works out for me, and if Russ gets elected the first thing he'll do is take my badge. Heck, after this morning, I wouldn't be surprised if Mayor Hickman asked me to resign."

"She would never do that. I know she thinks the world of you, and so do most of the people in this town. Don't leave. Let's talk."

But if Jet had learned anything in his life, it was when it was time to cut his losses and move on. He only wished he hadn't fallen so hard for Coco Grant. Then his leaving would be easy.

"If you could, please take care of Lily for a few more days until someone from Child Protective Services can pick her up. It might be easier for them to collect her, rather than me driving her over there. I can't seem to get around to doing that."

"But you still don't know if she's yours. You wouldn't

put her in foster care if she's yours. I know you couldn't do that."

"You don't know what I'm capable of doing."

It was tearing him apart to be so cold, so seemingly uncaring, but it was for Coco's own good, and it was especially for Lily's own good. He'd make a lousy dad, and obviously he wasn't very dependable or they would never have been locked in that jail cell. He deserved to be fired, and if he wasn't, he was thinking of handing in his resignation.

"Yes, I do. I know you're a loving man with a heart that's probably breaking right now, but you're also a stubborn man. I wish there was something I could say to change your mind."

"There isn't. Thanks for taking care of Lily. It would be better if she stayed with you. No telling what might befall her if she stays with me."

Secretly, he knew it would kill him to give her to the authorities, so he would do anything to avoid participating in that transfer.

He picked up his bag and backpack, and headed for the door.

As he came closer to Coco, she said, "Sure, I'll take care of Lily. But, Jet, you need to know one thing. In that jail, I fell in love with you, and for what it's worth, I've had more fun with you in the last few days than I've had with any man in my entire life. If you want to throw all of that away because of some misguided notion that you don't belong anywhere, let me say that you belong with me and with Lily. We want you to stay."

His throat tightened, and for a second or two he thought about dropping his bags and taking her in his arms.

But then he remembered the humiliation he'd caused her that morning, and the retaliation from Russ and possibly the entire town that was bound to come his way, and hers, for that matter.

"I can't," he told her, moisture filling his eyes.

He walked right past her, and Lily, then he was out the door, once again leaving behind everything he loved.

Chapter Ten

Of all the complaints Sheriff Wilson could get, he certainly didn't want to hear about the disturbing noise level coming from the Knightly estate. He thought he could merely call over to Russ's mansion and remind him that Briggs had a noise level ordinance after midnight, and this would be his second violation in six months. He hoped that phone call would be the end of it, but no. It was now almost 1:30 a.m. and it seemed as if the neighbors were upset en masse now.

He'd had his fill of Russ Knightly and for the past day and a half had been brooding about the embarrassment at the jail. He and Coco had exchanged a few text messages about Lily, but other than that, they'd kept their distance. He simply didn't know what his next move should be, and apparently, neither did she.

He and Nash would have no choice but to drive themselves over to the estate, a task he dreaded.

"Look at it this way," Nash told him as the two men hiked up to the front door of the sprawling estate. "This may be your very last duty as sheriff."

The estate sat on several acres of good open ranch

land, with a view of the Teton Mountain Range. The house itself was a modern two-story gray-and-white brick-and-mortar monster that never fit into the surrounding landscape. No doubt purposely constructed to stand out in a town of mostly redwood-cabin-type homes and a few late-nineteenth-century Victorians. Although Jet had never seen the inside of the Knightly mansion or been on the property, he knew it had both an outdoor and an indoor swimming pool, six bedrooms, a full-size bar, a movie theater that sat fifty people and a two-lane bowling alley.

The only good thing about the place was that its black metal fence only went around the back of the property. The front door had access to the street, so Jet and Nash didn't have to wait for some massive gate to open before they went in.

"Is that supposed to make me feel better?" Jet asked, obviously missing the irony of the situation that apparently Nash could see.

"Yeah, gives you that short-timer's attitude. By tomorrow night, we'll know who the new mayor will be, and if it's Russ, we can both probably kiss our jobs goodbye."

He had a point, but Jet wasn't in the mood to adopt it.

"Believe me, I know all about that attitude and all it does is get you into trouble," Jet said.

Nash chewed on that notion. "Okay, let's change this up. Are you committed to the town of Briggs and all those who live here? And as such, do you want to hang on to this job?"

"Yes," Jet responded without giving it any thought, an honest reaction that came from his very soul. He really did want to keep his job and stay right here in Briggs.

"Even if Russ wins?"

"I don't want him to win. I'm hoping this town comes to its collective senses and votes for Mayor Hickman."

"Then you need a new strategy."

"What's that?"

"What's that adage? If you give someone enough rope he'll hang himself? I'm thinking we need to take that approach tonight. Russ is arrogant enough to do his own hanging if we provide the rope. He won't see it coming."

Jet stared at Nash for a few seconds, thinking that this young man might be on to something.

"Follow my lead," Jet told him.

"I'm right with you," Nash said, adjusting his cowboy hat on his head as if he was getting ready for a physical battle and didn't want to worry about the hat falling off.

The two men were decked out in their dark brown uniforms, but both wore black cowboy boots and their own favorite hats. Nash had his black cowboy hat with the blue beaded band, and Jet wore his chocolate-colored handmade hat, one of the very first ones he'd purchased once he was on his own and making money. The hat symbolized his independence, and never was that more important to him than right now.

After ringing the bell several times, the door finally opened and the blonde Jet had seen kissing Russ while he was over in Jackson Hole stood on the other side. She wore a short, slinky purple dress and no shoes, her long hair draped her shoulders, and bright red lipstick accentuated her thin lips. "Can I help you?"

The music was deafening now that the door had been opened.

Jet nodded. "Got a call from the neighbors. Is Mr. Knightly in? We'd like to talk to him."

"He sure is. Come on in!" she said, her voice high with excitement. From what he could see, the Russ Knightly for Mayor gang was already celebrating the man's victory. Signs and banners were everywhere. A hundred or so people mulled around the big open room that soared in front of Jet, decorated with modern white furniture against pure white walls.

At the far end of the room, standing next to the floor-to-ceiling bank of windows, was the man of the hour, Russ Knightly, looking ready for bear when the Jackson Hole blonde was whispering news of the sheriff's visit.

Russ, dressed in a striped brown shirt and brown dress pants, immediately made his way to the door, after he scooped up a woman on either side of him. The Jackson Hole blonde being one of them. The other woman looked like a carbon copy of the blonde only with auburn hair.

Russ began talking as he approached. "If you've come to wish me well on the election tomorrow to try to butter me up so you can keep your job, Sheriff Wilson, you're too late. I'm already drawing up the paperwork to terminate you. I have several candidates in mind to take your place, candidates who I know for certain will do a much better job than you ever could."

Jet knew Russ was trying to get a rise out of him, but Jet knew how to curb his emotions in situations like these. He never flinched and never backed down.

"We're here because your neighbors are upset about the noise. It's going on 2:00 a.m., well past the midnight deadline for the local ordinance. I'm officially asking you to turn the volume down," Jet told him succinctly.

Russ smirked while still holding on to the women. "I'm going to change that stupid law so they should start getting used to it."

"Whether or not you'll change it has yet to be determined. Right now, the law requires you to cease and desist. And because this is your second notice in the last six months, I can confiscate your equipment and put you under arrest for disturbing the peace."

That was a bit of a stretch, but Jet wasn't in the mood for games. He was tired, and had had it with Russ's belligerent attitude.

"Ha!" Russ turned to his group and shouted, "The sheriff and his deputy here say we have to turn down the music or he can arrest me."

The music instantly stopped. Suddenly all eyes were on Jet Wilson and his deputy.

Russ turned back to the sheriff. "Is that better?"

"Yes, thank you, and please don't turn it on again tonight. We don't want to come back here."

"Well, I certainly wouldn't want to do anything to cause any trouble."

Nash said, "That's probably a wise decision on your part."

"Is that some kind of threat?"

"We would never threaten you, Mr. Knightly," Jet told him. "We're simply doing our job."

"What's with the Mr. Knightly crap?" Russ asked, resentment spilling over everything he said.

"Just showing you respect."

Russ laughed out loud, big deep belly laughs, so much so everyone in the room quit talking and paid close attention to what was going on at the door. Some of them pointed their phones at them, no doubt taking pictures and videos of the escalating situation. Russ let go of the two women and continued to laugh. "Respect? Oh, that's rich, after what happened yesterday morning at the jail."

Jet readied himself for what would likely happen next.

"That was an unfortunate circumstance that had nothing to do with you," Jet said.

And in the blink of an eye, Russ pulled back and threw a punch at Sheriff Jet Wilson. Jet ducked, and Russ socked Nash in the chin, causing him to fall back on his butt.

Within seconds almost everyone at the party had pulled out their phones, capturing the events in videos and pictures as Sheriff Wilson cuffed the potential mayor in front of all his potential voters.

"What was that you said about enough rope?" Jet said to Nash under his breath as the two men escorted Russ to their official SUV. Nash read Russ his rights, then they showed Russ the back seat. All the while the mayoral candidate was yelling about how his lawyer would bring them both down and how they were finished in this town.

Jet shut the back door, blocking out Russ's explosive diatribe of hateful rhetoric.

"Just wish you hadn't been so quick to duck, Sheriff. The guy packs a solid punch!" Nash rubbed his jaw, which was already turning bright red. "Have to admit I didn't think *following your lead* would land me on my backside."

"Frankly, neither did I. But it's a good reminder of how dangerous our job is. His fist could just as easily have been a hidden weapon that he attacked us with."

Nash said something else, but Jet was imagining a much darker scenario…one where it wasn't a fist that had hit Nash in the jaw, but something much more deadly.

Without further hesitation, Jet immediately called Marsha Oberlin at Child Protective Services and left her a message to come and get Lily. It was time to end this thing. Lily deserved a decision.

As Coco arrived at the Briggs Community Center to cast her vote for the new mayor, rumors were flying. Coco thought she'd be the topic of those rumors, along with Sheriff Jet Wilson and how they'd gotten trapped inside the jail cell. She expected that the talk of the town would be filled with snickering, scoffing and possible insults about how she and the sheriff had not only humiliated themselves, but humiliated Russ Knightly, who would most certainly be the new mayor by now.

She braced herself when the biggest town gossip came right for her as she entered the building. Even holding on to Lily in her cozy sling wouldn't protect her, nor would walking in with her hero brother, Carson, by her side. She'd called and asked him to join her.

Nope, Phyllis Gabaur was headed straight at her with a look of absolute disgust on her face…of course, Phyllis was always wearing that expression, even when she was happy, but it seemed intensified just then.

"Hang on to me," Coco whispered to her brother, who looked like his usual handsome self in a brown cowboy hat, a black wool parka, jeans and dusty work boots. He'd been over at M&M Riding School, teaching kids how to ride, a job he loved.

"I'm right here to run interference. Let me handle this," Carson said as Coco threaded her arm through his. She could always depend on Carson to get her through whatever came her way…all her sisters could. He had always been their fearless champion, defending them against anyone and anything that tried to bring them down.

"Mrs. Gabaur, nice to see you again," Carson said, tipping his hat in her direction.

She ignored him and looked at Coco, as if he wasn't even there. "I hope you're not voting for that scoundrel Russ Knightly. Serves him right if nobody voted for him given how he treated our sheriff last night for simply doing his job. And what of Deputy Sheriff Young? They're saying he lost two teeth over the matter. That Knightly shouldn't be mayor of anything, much less of our fair city of Briggs. We deserve better. We deserve another four years of Mayor Sally Hickman, an upstanding, honest mayor who abides by the laws and doesn't flaunt them. A vote for Sally Hickman is a vote for Idaho values."

Then she handed both Carson and Coco large buttons that featured Mayor Hickman's smiling face and walked to the next voter behind Coco, beginning the same speech all over again.

"What was that all about?" Carson asked in a hushed voice.

"I don't have a clue," she replied, scanning the center.

Carson and Coco needed to get their ballots. They walked over to Hank Marsh and his wife. There were a few other proposed laws on the ballot that the townsfolk were voting on. Like whether or not the city should add another holiday to the already packed roster. There was a petition for an official Spud Day to coincide with all the Spud events that happened over at the fairgrounds every year in the early fall.

Still, in spite of the other issues that the good people of Briggs would be voting on, deciding who would be mayor of the city was the biggest.

"Mornin', Carson. Doctor Grant," Hank said as he handed each of them a ballot.

"How's that little baby doing?" Dottie Marsh asked.

"Just fine. Thanks for asking," she said.

"Can I get a peek at her?" Dottie wanted to know.

"Sure, but can you tell me what's going on with Russ? Did something happen?"

"You don't know? I thought for sure…because of the sheriff…and you. Mr. Knightly spent the night in jail for punching Deputy Sheriff Nash Young in the face. Apparently, it was pretty bad. I don't like to gossip, but I heard the deputy might have to get dentures."

"What? I don't believe that."

"It's what everybody's talking about. People even videoed it on their phones."

Hank and the others filled Coco and Carson in on the rest of the details. It seemed everyone's focus was squarely on Russ's shoulders and his wild punch.

And not only that, if Russ thought he had the title of mayor locked up, he was wrong. Sally Hickman was going to give him a real run for his money, which meant that Jet would probably be able to keep his job…if he wanted it.

The problem was, after everything Jet had told her the last time he was at her house, Coco didn't know if staying in Briggs was something Jet Wilson would ever truly consider.

WHEN JET SPOTTED Coco and Carson exiting the community center, everything in him had to be forced to shut down. He could barely keep his eyes off her, the soft curve of her features, the way her hair framed her face, the way she walked with a confident step, which made her hips sway sweetly, the way the corners of her mouth tilted up as if she were always happy, the way she loved to carry Lily around in that sling that swept across her chest, keeping Lily warm and safe next to Coco's body.

He took in a deep breath and slowly let it out, thinking about the curves and edges that made Coco Grant. Heck, he even loved her pretty toes painted a soft pink. There wasn't one thing about her—her great disposition, how smart she was, how considerately she treated Lily and all those critters she took in without giving it a second thought—that he didn't love.

He had it bad for Doctor Coco Grant and just seeing her again broke his heart. He truly didn't know how he would ever get over her or Lily, who he'd also fallen in love with that very first night.

"She's under your skin, and for the life of me, I can't see what's keeping you from settling down with that fine woman. I know she's all about wanting to be with you, but you're suddenly playing hard to get. You want to talk about it?" Nash asked as they both jumped into the SUV. Fortunately, they'd missed out on crossing paths with Coco after they voted—for Sally Hickman, of course.

"I don't want to talk about it," Jet said as he stuck the key into the ignition, backed out of the parking space and drove away.

"Well, I do. I want to know what's going on with you."

"None of your business."

Jet's phone vibrated as it sat on the dashboard, where he could see who was calling. It was Marsha Oberlin from Child Protective Services. He'd already received a couple calls from her, but in the light of day, he had decided he wasn't ready to speak to her, after all.

"But it is my business after I've taken a punch for you. You owe me big-time and this is how you can pay me back. Tell me what's going on in that ornery head of yours and why you're not talking to your girlfriend."

"She's not my girlfriend."

"Oh? You could'a fooled me. She sure looked like your girlfriend yesterday morning inside that jail cell. Yes, siree…she was absolutely no longer Russ Knightly's girlfriend, that's for sure."

Jet hated when Nash wouldn't give up on a subject.

"I don't want to talk about it."

"You said that already and obviously it has no effect on me. I'm here to listen. I'm a good listener. Even Drew says I am, and she should know, she's one of the best listeners in town."

Jet drove them the next couple of miles in silence until they reached the station. Russ had long since gone home after his lawyer had him released bright and early that morning.

He and Nash sat at their respective desks before Jet said another word. "Doctor Grant deserves better than me. I'm not the kind of man who can remain in one spot. Something always happens to mess it up. I don't want to get her hopes up. Heck, I don't want to get my hopes up. Every time I do…well, it never works out."

Nash let out a slow breath. "You're kidding, right?"

Jet gazed at him. "No. I'm not kidding."

Nash sat back in his chair, stuck his feet up on his desk and slipped his hat over his face. "Tell you what. When you've got something to say that makes sense, wake me up, 'cause right now you're so full of nonsense, it's—"

"I'm spilling my guts to you and you're going to sleep?"

"You sound like you're still a kid trapped in the system," Nash murmured from under his hat. "Wake up, Jet Wilson. Those days are over. Just like last night with Russ. You were in control, not him. You get to choose your next move, and if you want Coco Grant, and that little baby that's probably yours, you have to fight for both of them. As it is you're not looking like much of a fighter. Didn't all those years, good and bad, teach you anything? Listen, my dad was an alcoholic for most of my childhood. We all have our own stuff to deal with. But the secret is to deal with it. Not sweep it under the rug, and not use it to shield us when something is tough. At least, that's what my mom would tell me, and believe me, she dealt with a lot from me and my four brothers."

"You have four brothers?"

Nash sat up a bit, taking his hat off and resting it

brim up on his desk. "Yep, and each one was worse than the last."

"My heart goes out to your mom for having to deal with the likes of you, and your brothers," Jet said. He rose from his desk and pushed Nash's feet off his as he walked over to the small basket that caught all their mail next to the door. "You make a lot of sense for a man who doesn't know when to duck."

Nash grinned. "That was all your fault. You should've stopped him with your manly shoulders and mean sheriff ways."

"I told you to follow my lead," Jet said. "You saw me duck."

Jet rifled through the mail until he stopped on a letter addressed to him from the lab in Boise. His heart raced as he stared at what had to be the results of his DNA test. Of all the days for it to arrive, this had to be the worst.

"I'll keep that in mind next time."

Suddenly, Jet's entire focus narrowed to that letter and what it could mean for him, Lily…and Coco, too.

Then, as if he'd been hit by lightning, or a light had gone on inside his head, he knew exactly what he wanted to do…what he needed to do…and nothing else mattered.

"Good idea, Nash, and, hey, thanks for the advice. I knew there was a reason I was keeping your sorry self on the payroll."

"Anytime."

"Don't let it go to your head. You're still only a deputy."

"That's for dang sure," Nash said, cupping his very bruised chin.

Jet's phone vibrated in his pocket. Everything seemed to be coming at him at warp speed and he didn't know if he was completely ready for the onslaught as he contemplated his future.

When he looked at the screen he saw that it was from Coco. For a second, he didn't want to answer and instead wanted to speak to her in person, but then something told him he should take the call.

"Coco? Are you home? I want to stop by."

"Hi, Jet. Yes, and you better get over to my place fast. Marsha Oberlin is here from Child Protective Services and she wants to take Lily. I don't think I can stop her. She said she's called you several times, but you're not picking up. What's going on? Jet?"

"Stall her. Whatever you do, don't let her take Lily."

THE GOOD THING about living in a small town was that whenever you needed the townsfolk to help, it only required a couple calls and everyone for miles circled their wagons to support you.

That was what happened once Coco called Drew. Within what Coco could only describe as minutes, a bevy of people, the same ones who had donated all the baby things days before, along with a few more, showed up at her clinic to waylay Ms. Oberlin as best they could. Their arsenal? Cakes, cookies, more baby supplies and a barrage of questions about fostering and what Lily could expect.

Not that Coco believed that anything they put forward would deter this woman from doing her job. But it helped, for instance, when Amanda Gump offered to send the woman home with several dozen tasty treats from Holy Rollers for the kids in her charge in Idaho Falls. Fortunately, Ms. Oberlin couldn't turn down the offer and followed Amanda out the front door. Amanda also told a little lie about how Sheriff Wilson and Lily were at Holy Rollers then, taking a much-needed break.

Actually, baby Lily was fast asleep in her bassinet on Coco's bed.

The crowd trooped after Amanda and Marsha Oberlin. Just in the nick of time, too, because the very next moment, Lily woke up with a start, protesting all the commotion. Before Coco went into the bedroom to get her, she slipped one of the premade bottles in the electric warmer so it would be ready for Lily once she was fully awake. Lily didn't like to wait when she was hungry.

Coco then went to her bedroom to hold that little darling, wondering if this would be the last time she ever cradled her. As soon as she picked up Lily, she stopped crying.

"There's my big girl," Coco purred, then hummed "Happy Birthday" to her.

Coco carefully placed her on her shoulder, her little head bobbing as Lily tried to lift it. She had that sweet baby smell, and her skin felt like silk. Coco's love for her was all-consuming, and having to give her up was tearing her apart.

Lily began cooing with the sound of Coco's voice and her touch. "Did you have a good sleep, my darling? I bet you did, and now you're hungry. Well, I've got a bottle warming just for you."

Coco loved holding Lily, and fussing over her. She loved how she felt in her arms and how her little eyes were beginning to focus and how Lily would try to talk whenever Coco played with her. They had a rhythm going, the two of them, and having Marsha Oberlin close by bothered her more than she could have anticipated.

She had no idea how she was ever going to let Lily go and had even thought about maybe adopting her, or start out by being her foster parent. Coco had already begun the paperwork online. Just because Jet could let her go, didn't mean that Coco would, as well. Lily meant so much to her now, no way would she allow some stranger to take her.

"Not on my watch," Coco told Lily as she stroked her silky round head.

"Nor on mine," Jet said from behind her. Coco whirled around to see Jet standing in her bedroom doorway, his hat in his hand, still wearing his overcoat.

"You came."

"Did you doubt that I would?"

"Not this time. They want to take Lily. The woman said that you called her."

"I was confused. Calling her was a mistake that I deeply regret."

"What do we do now? I don't want to give her up."

"Neither do I."

Coco's eyes watered. "But what if she's not yours? Will you still fight to keep her?"

"Yes."

Coco couldn't help but smile .

"Why the change of heart?" she asked.

"I realized that I love her and I love you. I was scared to admit it. Scared that you didn't feel the same way and once again I'd have to steel my emotions."

"What's giving you the courage to say all of this now?"

"Because I know what I want, and it's you and Lily and I'm willing to fight for you both. I'm so very sorry for what I said yesterday and how I acted. I was such a fool. Can you ever forgive me?"

Coco could no longer stop the tears that spilled down her cheeks. She loved Jet Wilson more than she could put into words.

"I forgave you as soon as I heard your voice," she said.

They fell into each other's arms, and kissed while Lily cooed on Coco's shoulder.

Drew entered the room, clearing her throat, announcing that she'd arrived. "We tried our best to keep Ms. Oberlin away," she said, "but as soon as she realized you and the baby weren't at Holy Rollers, she marched right back here. She'll be here any second."

"Well, tell her she can't have Lily," Jet said, pulling an envelope out of his coat pocket then handing it to Coco. "She's mine."

She stared at the envelope. "But this isn't even open. How do you know what it says?"

"I always knew, but couldn't face it. Now I can. Open it."

Coco hesitated. "I...can't."

Jet took it back and ripped open the envelope, and there in no uncertain terms were the results. Baby Lily and Jet Wilson shared the same DNA.

"Sheriff Wilson, I do believe you're a father," Coco said after looking at the letter and handing it to Drew, who left the room with it.

Jet smiled and opened his arms. "But will you be her mother?"

Coco nodded. "Yes. A thousand times yes."

Lily began to fuss, and Jet held them, stroking the baby's head. "It's okay, sweetheart," he told her. "You're safe now."

And with that, they would each swear for years to come that baby Lily giggled.

Epilogue

Three weeks later

Jet Wilson pulled his SUV to a stop outside the Grants' ranch house knowing perfectly well this was the beginning of many Sunday family dinners that would now be a welcome part of his life. It was something he'd dreamed about and longed for, and to think that it was becoming a reality after all this time was almost more than he could bear.

He was going to get the full, honest-to-goodness family experience—and he hoped it would be a forever one—where members stuck around, no matter what. And he could put down roots knowing he wouldn't be "moving on" like he had his whole life.

"It's going to be okay," Coco told him as she squeezed his shoulder, glancing into the back seat to see that Lily was waking up, her big eyes looking around as though trying to figure out exactly where she was. "I know you're nervous about telling my family we're engaged, but don't be. They already love you as the town sheriff, Jet, and I know they're going to love you and welcome you and Lily as part of the family."

"That's what scares me the most. Me, big tough sheriff, and look at me, I'm scared of having your family reject me. That I might say or do something wrong…that it won't be true, that it won't be what I'd always dreamed… It's just weird for me, that's all." Again, he had the thought of how grateful he was that he could be totally honest with this woman and how reassuring that was.

"It's Thanksgiving. There'll be so many people at dinner, even if you did say or do something silly, not that you will…but if you did, nobody would notice. I promise you. And besides, Lily and I are your family now, and we'll always be here for you. And we know you'll always be here for us, too."

He turned to look at her. In the fading light she was even more beautiful than he ever thought possible. "Do you know how much I love you?"

She nodded. "As much as I love you. Now let's go in and enjoy the evening. Dinner won't start until everyone is seated. Rules of the house."

Just then Mayor Sally Hickman and her husband parked next to them. Sally had won the mayor's race by a landslide, shutting Russ out completely. Last thing Jet had heard about Russ Knightly was that he'd put his estate up for sale and moved to Jackson Hole for good.

"The mayor is here?"

"Longtime friend of the family."

"I had no idea."

"There's a lot you don't know about the Grants."

"And now I have all the time in the world to learn."

"Yes, you do. Shall we go in?"

"Not before we kiss."

He leaned over and pressed his lips to hers. Warm and inviting. It always amazed him how each time they kissed he felt her love and passion race through his body, matching a surge of happiness and that unmistakable feeling of completeness. He had a hunch… one so strong that he didn't doubt it…that it would always be like this between them. His wish, his dream, had come true—a woman who loved him, a child to cherish forever and an extended family to welcome him into their folds.

When he and Coco pulled apart, she said, "I love you, Sheriff Jet Wilson, and I can't wait to be your wife."

"Maybe we should elope."

"Can't. My family hates to miss a wedding…and speaking of weddings, we should probably have a small one. Something always goes wrong when my family plans for a big wedding. It never seems to go off right the first time."

"Well, we already have the license and isn't Father Beau coming to dinner?"

"What are you saying?"

Jet knew it was a crazy idea. One that he could never have imagined just a few weeks ago, but it was an idea that made perfect sense now. Why not?

"In order to make sure nothing goes awry at our wedding, Doctor Coco Grant, will you marry me now? Tonight? Before dinner? All your family and, from what you've told me about your parents, most of your friends are probably already inside. Why don't we use this night to officially start our lives together? I have a feeling Lily would like it if we did, and I know for certain that I would. So, my love, will you marry me, right here, right now?"

A wide grin spread across her lovely face. "Why, Sheriff Wilson, you couldn't have made me any happier. Yes, I will marry you right here and right now."

"You will?"

"I will. Everything about our relationship has been spontaneous from the beginning. Why should we change it?"

"Okay then. But how do you think your family will take to this?"

"Are you kidding?" She beamed at him.

So, in the hour that followed, while the turkey browned in the oven, and those good Idaho potatoes boiled in a pot, he, Jet Wilson and Coco Grant exchanged wedding vows in front of her entire family, many friends, including Drew—who instantly became Coco's maid of honor—Drew's parents and Nash Young—who stepped up, of course, to play the part as best man. All the while baby Lily stared wide-eyed at the loving couple from Mildred Grant's arms.

"I now pronounce you husband and wife," Father Beau said. "You may kiss the bride."

And with that, the group erupted with hoots and good wishes, as baby Lily tried her best to add her own voice to the resounding glee in the room.

* * * * *

*If you enjoyed this cowboy romance from
USA* Today *bestselling author Mary Leo, check out
these other titles in her* BRIGGS, IDAHO *series,
available from www.Harlequin.com!*

*FALLING FOR THE COWBOY
AIMING FOR THE COWBOY
CHRISTMAS WITH THE RANCHER
HER FAVORITE COWBOY
A CHRISTMAS WEDDING FOR THE COWBOY
A COWBOY IN HER ARMS
A COWBOY TO KISS*

COMING NEXT MONTH FROM

HARLEQUIN®

Western Romance

Available November 7, 2017

#1665 A TEXAS SOLDIER'S CHRISTMAS
Texas Legacies: The Lockharts
by Cathy Gillen Thacker
Soldier Zane Lockhart rushes home to Texas to claim his son, then discovers Nora Caldwell's adopted baby isn't his. He still wants to make the army nurse and her boy family—in time for baby Liam's first Christmas!

#1666 THE COWBOY SEAL'S CHRISTMAS BABY
Cowboy SEALs • by Laura Marie Altom
When former navy SEAL Gideon Snow finds a baby and a woman with amnesia on a remote Arizona trail, he's forced to take them home. Christmas at his ranch just got more interesting!

#1667 A SNOWBOUND COWBOY CHRISTMAS
Saddle Ridge, Montana • by Amanda Renee
Single mom-to-be Emma Sheridan has one job: convince Dylan Slade to sell his Montana guest ranch. But when Emma is stuck in Saddle Ridge, she realizes she likes being snowbound with the handsome rancher.

#1668 THE BULL RIDER'S PLAN
Montana Bull Riders • by Jeannie Watt
Jess Hayward is off on a rodeo road trip, where he plans to fulfill his bull-riding dream. But he doesn't expect Emma Sullivan, his best friend's sister, to tag along. She's a distraction he doesn't need!

YOU CAN FIND MORE INFORMATION ON UPCOMING HARLEQUIN® TITLES, FREE EXCERPTS AND MORE AT WWW.HARLEQUIN.COM.

HWESTCNM1017

Beckett finally spoke. "Uh, what seems to be the trouble?"

His voice had an odd, strangled note to it. Was he
laughing at her? When she couldn't see him, Ella couldn't
be quite sure. "It's stuck in my hair comb. I don't want
to rip the sweater—or yank out my hair, for that matter."

He paused again, then she felt the air stir as he moved
closer. The scent of him was stronger now, masculine and
outdoorsy, and everything inside her sighed a welcome.

He stood close enough that she could feel the heat
radiating from him. She caught her breath, torn between
a completely prurient desire for the moment to last at
least a little longer and a wild hope that the humiliation
of being caught in this position would be over quickly.

"Hold still," he said. Was his voice deeper than usual?
She couldn't quite tell. She did know it sent tiny delicious
shivers down her spine.

"You've really done a job here," he said after a
moment.

"I know. I'm not quite sure how it tangled so badly."

She would have to breathe soon or she was likely to pass out. She forced herself to inhale one breath and then another until she felt a little less light-headed.

"Almost there," he said, his big hands in her hair, then a moment later she felt a tug and the sweater slipped all the way over her head.

"There you go."

"Thank you." She wanted to disappear, to dive under that great big log bed and hide away. Instead, she forced her mouth into a casual smile. "These Christmas sweaters can be dangerous. Who knew?"

She was blushing. She could feel her face heat and wondered if he noticed. This certainly counted among the most embarrassing moments of her life.

"Want to explain again what you're doing in my bedroom, tangled up in your clothes?" he asked.

She frowned at his deliberately risqué interpretation of something that had been innocent. Mostly.

There had been that secret moment when she had closed her eyes and imagined being here with him under that soft quilt, but he had no way of knowing that.

She folded up her sweater, wondering if she would ever be able to look the man in the eye again.

Don't miss
THE RANCHER'S CHRISTMAS SONG
by RaeAnne Thayne,
available November 2017 wherever
Harlequin® Special Edition books and ebooks are sold.

www.Harlequin.com

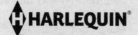

LOVE
Harlequin
romance?

Join our Harlequin community to share your thoughts and connect with other romance readers!

Be the first to find out about promotions, news, and exclusive content!

Sign up for the Harlequin e-newsletter and download a free book from any series at

www.TryHarlequin.com

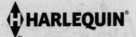

Looking for inspiration in tales
of hope, faith and heartfelt romance?

Check out **Love Inspired**®,
Love Inspired® **Suspense** and
Love Inspired® **Historical** books!

New books available every month!

CONNECT WITH US AT:

www.LoveInspired.com

Harlequin.com/Community

 Facebook.com/LoveInspiredBooks

Twitter.com/LoveInspiredBooks

www.ReaderService.com